Faerie Wishes

Beyond the Faerie Wall

Michelle Helen Fritz, E.A. Shanniak

Clear Spring Books LLC

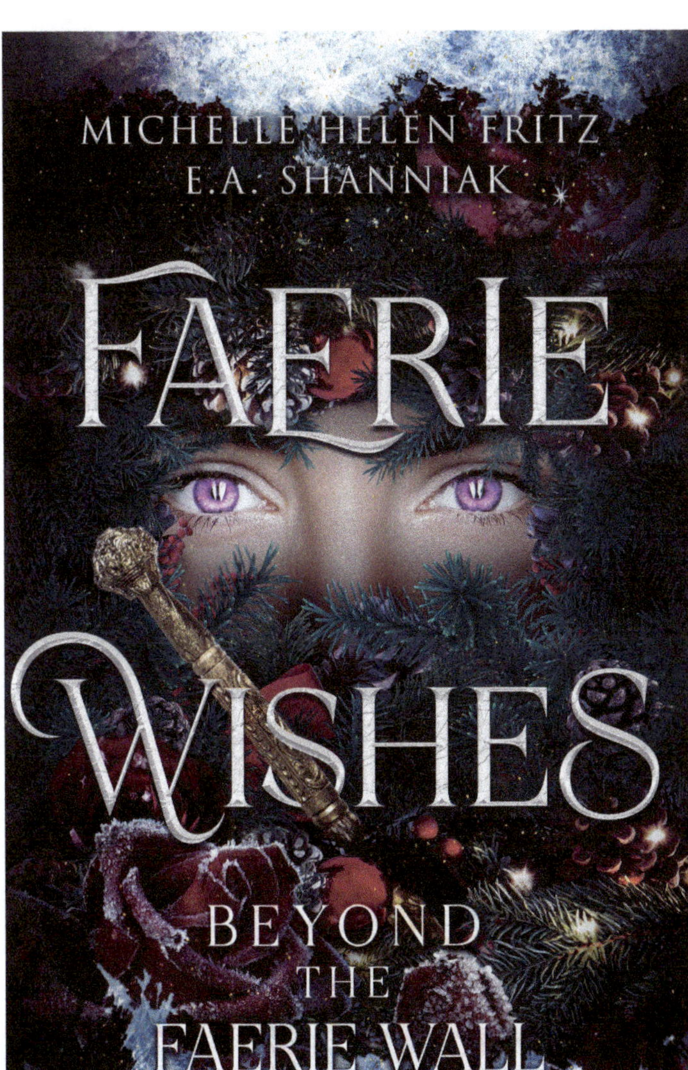
MICHELLE HELEN FRITZ
E.A. SHANNIAK
FAERIE
WISHES
BEYOND
THE
FAERIE WALL

Faerie Wishes: Beyond the Faerie Wall by Michelle Helen Fritz

Featuring: E.A. Shanniak

Chapter Heading Art: Michelle Helen Fritz

Cover Design: Wanderlust Ink & Tome LLC

Edmund & Faetilda Character Art: Samaiya Art

Formatting: E.A. Shanniak

Proofreading: Cathey N.

Published by Clear Spring Books LLC of Clear Spring, MD

Dedication

from Michelle Helen Fritz

For Faeriedust who I shall always carry in my heart. Fly freely among the clouds and dance amidst the twinkling star dust.

Contents

Chapter One

Unholy Night

For the proud proprietor of Faerie Wishes, an up-and-coming toy shoppe located in the foggy streets of London, there was no greater joy than seeing the light in a child's eye as they beheld one of his creations. Last autumn, at three and forty years of age, Mister Edmund Smithe had sold his farm and was finally ready to open his shoppe for longer hours, just in time for the wintertide hustle and bustle. The merry man has long been selling his wares from the confines of his barn in Derbyshire, and when pressed if he ever dreamed of opening his establishment, he would always deny the claim. His toys were for those near and dear to him until a peddler bought a few of his wooden rocking horses and returned a fortnight later to tell Edmund how marvelous his toys were received in London. The seed of desire to see his playthings in the hands of more children grew until the tasks of running his dairy farm failed to bring him joy. And so, he did the only thing that he could: he sold the farm, which had been in his family's name for generations, and relocated into London.

A little girl with the biggest smile was looking in at Mr. Smithe through the elegant scroll of Faerie Wishes printed across the large bay window. Waving goodbye to the little girl, Edmund's heart warmed, and he felt satisfaction traveling all the way to his soul as he sighed with contentment. The doll, which was wrapped in the girl's arms, would bring many delightful days of companionship to her new friend. The swivel neck and carved ears of the doll were a new design. Everyone who spied those features were in awe of his creation. With Christmastide upon them, he had been surprised by the purchase, but the nanny hadn't seemed to bat an eye at the price. He took a moment to watch as the child and nurserymaid disappeared from his sight into a mix of swirling snowflakes. The weather had turned colder in the last few days, and now, a wintertide slush coated the outside in a wonderland of white, glittering like the sequins of a lady's dress. Was there anything more refreshing than falling snow? It enlivened the senses and made the mind clearer. Edmund discovered early evenings spent around his toasty fireplace always inspired new designs for his toys, even if, at times, the extra moisture in the air made his bones ache. At four and forty, he wasn't a young fellow. Most days, he suffered an odd sharp ache in his left leg, and whenever he stood over his work table for too long, his back pained him. But such was the life of a trade worker.

Edmund rounded his wooden counter and strolled through his shoppe toward the door. Reaching out his hand, he twisted the lock and heard the tumblers engage. Rotating the sign from open to closed, he turned on his heel and moved past hanging puppets, ornate doll houses, a display of jump ropes, battledore, shuttlecock, pewter figures of toy soldiers, and many other darling creations that caused his lips to curl into a grin. He ran a hand through his short-cropped brown hair that was flecked with a touch of gray, then visited each lantern in his shoppe to snuff out the rippling orange flame.

His stomach rumbled. It was well past dinner time, and bread, cheese, and ale awaited him upstairs in his living compartments. He was eager to consume the fare so he could begin sketching his idea for a new invention. Then, there were requests awaiting his attention. It was the holiday season, and customers had placed orders that needed to be completed. There was much work to be done, and it pleased him so much. Edmund whistled a jolly tune as he ascended the staircase.

Kerplunk! Rattletrap! Bam!

It was the third thump that finally wrested Edmund from slumber. He was disoriented and quite put out that his dreams of winning *'Best Toy Shoppe in the Greater London Area'* from the ToyMaker's Guild had been obliterated with the offending noise. *Noise?* Edmund gripped the navy coverlet tightly against his chest and blinked to clear the haze from his mind as his ears strained to pick up any disturbance. Living above his shoppe in the city meant it wasn't unusual to hear the odd sound or clattering racket. Even the rats ran amuck at night, chased by the determined felines who longed to fill their empty bellies. But never had he been awakened with dread that someone was breaking into his establishment. What could he do?

Thwack, wack, and *kerplunk* peppered the air in rapid succession, causing Edmund to toss his blanket aside and leap to his bare feet. Quickly dropping to his knees, he extended his arm and reached under his bed. When his fingers brushed against the wooden bat, he leaned forward and wrapped his digits around the handle. A quiet *huzzah* left his lips as he straightened and tiptoed to his closed bedchamber door. As silently as possible, he twisted the doorknob. When the creak from the hinges rent the air, he cringed, and a shiver danced along his spine. He waited a moment to see if a foe would charge up the wooden stairs to vanquish him or, at the very least, clobber him over the head. Looking up, he saw the tail of his nightcap twisted at an odd angle, which was the least of his problems at the moment.

Further widening the opening, Edmund crept from his room and proceeded to carefully place a foot down onto each step. He knew which stairs to avoid and where each weak spot was located. Edmund didn't need any light to illuminate the darkness that shrouded his movements. Once he descended the stairs, he saw a glow from under the back room's dark curtain separating the shoppe from the work area. The wooden floorboards glowed from the candlelight, and displayed the shadows of creatures lurking behind the curtain barrier. Movement behind the fabric stilled his thundering heart; his breath hitched. Sounds of grumbling speech reached his ears, and his brows careened together in confusion. He couldn't quite make out the rambling words, which seemed guttural and harsh. *What manner of speech is this?* he wondered as he swallowed. His mouth was dry. Edmund drew in a slow breath and exhaled, digging deeply down into his core to locate the courage to interrupt their unsavory deeds. If they meant him harm, wouldn't they have found him by now and followed through on their dastardly plan?

Closing the space to the curtain, he raised a tentative hand and grabbed the material's edge. He quietly nudged a corner of the curtain aside, allowing him to get a glimpse of what was taking place on the other side. His jaw unhinged, and his eyes grew large at what was happening before him. Five, or maybe six, green-tinted creatures with bulbous snout-like noses and dark beady eyes held hammers, hand saws, and all the tools of his trade as they each turned their attention his way. When the largest of the bunch, who was no taller than Edmund's knee, growled at him, Edmund jumped back and nearly wet himself in haste to be as far away as possible from the night terrors. Was he dreaming? What, in all the world, were those creatures? Since arriving in London, he'd heard tales of *The Wall* and its inhabitants who weren't human and who employed trickery and harm to the mortals stupid enough to get too close or, heaven forbid, even cross the barrier. He'd never suspected *he'd* be *visited* by such creatures. How to get rid of the little beasts? More importantly, what were they doing with *his tools*? *His orders! His life's work!*

A pool of lava formed in his middle and surged through his veins, making stars dance across his vision. He must put a stop to their antics! They had no place in his shoppe! Edmund's lips pulled down; his eyes narrowed as he slung the curtain aside with a flourish and marched into the workspace.

Trolls! His eyes scanned their faces and noticed the warts and strings of spittle dangling from the corners of their mouths. They were utterly repulsive in their scantily dressed state; only loin cloths covered their naughty bits. Perhaps they were impervious to the chill in the air? The fire had been banked before he sought his bed, and the crispness crept up under his nightshirt as he absent-mindedly curled his toes, attempting to warm them.

When the creatures only stared at Edmund, he felt emboldened enough to venture further into the room. Slowly, one of the trolls held up a wooden creation, and Edmund peered at it as he made his way forward. The thing rested on the curved base of a rocking horse. While it did have the body of a horse, the head was of a terrifying dragon with razor-sharp teeth. Edmund sucked in a breath and grabbed the figure from the troll, holding it closer to his face. Was this the same ebony wood he'd paid dearly for in order to fulfill Lord Denbury's request? His heart skipped a beat; in fact, it skipped several beats, and his mouth hung slack-jawed as he tried to splutter out words. *How? Why?* His stomach wanted to revolt and cast up his meager dinner.

The troll smiled up at him as a snot bubble popped from its nose. The scene was bizarre, and a harsh guffaw flew from Edmund's mouth. Canting his head to the next troll, he noticed the doll he had set aside to glue a golden wig upon it in the morning. An avalanche of ice chilled the marrow of his bones. Now, from the doll's head, dangled threads of black, twisted fur. He could barely make out the cornflower blue eyes beneath the layer of gray paint now coating its entire porcelain head. The horrid thing resembled a rotting corpse. And he had been paid handsomely to create a beautiful playmate; he would never be able to fix this mess! Scrutinizing the oblong work table, he saw some sticky substance spilled over it and noted the upturned bottles of his most expensive paint seeping into the wood grain.

Debtors' prison! That is what awaited him! He would be in the poor house once it was discovered he couldn't make good on the orders he'd already accepted payment for. The ebony wood alone had cost a small fortune, and now, it was nothing more than rubbish. He felt tears prick his eyes. He had even received a request from the Queen herself, and he closed his eyes after he spied the doll house he had so lovingly crafted, now cut into small jagged pieces.

The most ridiculous part of this entire fiasco was that the trolls all seemed pleased by their wares. They might look like the ugliest monsters, but they didn't seem to purposefully be ruining his life. Perhaps beyond *The Wall,* these were treasures any faerieling would be thrilled to be gifted. But he wasn't in Faerie, and *they* didn't belong here in his realm.

Another troll approached him and tugged at his nightshirt. When Edmund looked down, he observed a soft body doll with cracks along its limbs and a huge chip where its chin once was. It had been dressed in some sort of a burlap sack with a rope tied around its center. The troll held it by the cord and spun it around over his head. Edmund had to take a step back to avoid being hit by it. Was this how trolls played?

Edmund didn't have the heart to clobber them over the head with his forgotten bat. They had already inflicted so much destruction to his livelihood. What would an hour or more of their creativity do to him? His scandalized eyes watched on as they continued to ruin his things. He regretted selling his dairy farm when the trolls threw their goods down atop the table and jumped to their feet. One at a time, each beast came before Edmund and saluted him before marching from the room and through the back exit of his establishment.

His wits had gone begging; he wasn't certain if they'd ever return. Had he just seen what he thought he had? Did trolls exist, or was he having some kind of a mental breakdown? Was Bedlam more of a fitting home than a debtors' prison? What Edmund most needed was sleep. Perhaps after a few hour's rest, he'd wake to discover his unholy night had been some wildly terrible nightmare.

His bare feet carried him to the door, and his free hand deftly secured the locks. However, what good they would do for him now remained to be seen. Still, there were mortal thieves in his realm, and they would be delighted to discover an unbolted way inside. They possibly possessed fewer scruples to deal him a fatal wound. Turning around, he kept his eyes downcast, not wanting to deny or confirm the troll's activities.

Trudging back up his staircase, he let the bat slip from his fingers to smack against the floor. Crawling into his bed, he pulled up the coverlet and tried to control his breathing so his body would stop quaking.

"Just a dream," Edmund murmured to himself as his eyelids slid closed.

Chapter Two

The Jingle of Bells

Faetilda flew under the jingling bells dangling from silver ribbons on the snowy tree branches. Normally, their merry tinkle would give her pause as she delighted in their peal ringing along the air. This evening, however, she couldn't enjoy much of anything. She pulled her scarlet pelisse tighter against her chest as she flew toward The Wall.

The mere sight of it gave her chills as a whirlwind of fear and doubt crept into her bones and made her heart race.

Every creature in Faerie avoided *The Wall*. Humans dwelled in their little homes and raised their boorish families on the other side. Their nasty, greedy fingers waited to clutch whatever they could grab just to possess it, and their disregard for nature sickened her. Faetilda scowled, hoping never to come across the dreadful beings. The Wall was constructed to keep the fae safe, fortified to withstand any human interference with whatever primitive weapons they had lately constructed. Mortals were the creators of destruction and ruin, and every faerieling learned that very lesson early on.

King Theron should've made The Wall taller, Faetilda thought, wringing her hands more vigorously the closer she came to the wall. She stopped and puffed her cheeks, blowing out a long breath as the cobbled wall stretched upward before her. She shook her hands out at her sides as if she was ridding herself of all doubts to fortify her resolve in her mission.

"Up and over," she encouraged herself. "Up and over and back in a jif." She stomped her foot. "Ohhh, bother! Why couldn't I have just said no when I was asked to watch over those heathens!"

Her best friend, Flora, had longed to adventure out on a sleigh ride with her new beau but couldn't find the time due to her duties. Being the best friend ever, Faetilda agreed to take Flora's position for just a handful of hours so she could go and enjoy herself. In all their long discussions, never once had she thought to ask Flora what it was that she was employed to do. They had both expressed joy in their tasks and that had been that. As far as Faetilda knew, Flora worked as a nurserymaid at a fae nursery school, not as the caregiver for *trolls*!

"Oh my stars and heavens," Faetilda said, dreading the climb up the structure since her wings wouldn't work quite as well once the magic of The Wall interfered. Flying was so much easier and faster, too. Her marvelous wings significantly cut down her traveling time.

Upon touching the stone fortification, she lost most of her ability to fly and use magic; almost anything magical was moot once crossing into the human world. Faetilda peeked behind her, seeing her shimmery, rose-gold wings still attached to her back, but just not as fluttery as she was accustomed to.

Faetilda hiked up the hem of her skirts and began the tedious process of finding foot and finger holds to help her ascend the fifty-foot high fortification. Her labored breaths escaped from her mouth in bursts of steam before her. When she felt as though she'd never reached the top, her hand came to rest along its edge. Pulling herself the rest of the way up, she swung one leg over, then the other, and sat atop the wall. Faetilda cautiously peered down the side, hoping to remain ambiguous to the cretinous humans. The journey down seemed to pass by at a quicker pace, and before she knew it, Faetilda landed on solid ground with a thud. Taking a step forward, she slipped on an icy stone and fell back onto her bottom. She scrambled to her feet, straightening her pelisse as she took stock of her translucent wings, giving them a hasty flutter that proved they were unharmed. Breathing out, and with a triumphant gleam, she raised a fist in the air. No human stone could bring her down!

Snow fell from the dark heavens onto her head, planting soft kisses on her fiery tresses. Her half-boots found purchase, and she felt confident sneaking along amidst the shadows.

Gaslamps glimmered under the glitter of falling snowflakes. Rich, burgundy brick buildings soared toward the sky. Wooden carved signs hung over the shoppe doors detailing the keepers' services and wares. Some shoppes sported beautiful white filigree writing, though they were far and few between. Tentatively, she strode forward, glancing all around her in hopes of spying on the runaway trolls and not *a human*. What she would do when faced with one...well, it didn't bear even thinking about.

The frightening stories she heard about them were enough to give Faetilda nightmares, no matter that she was no longer a faerieling. Horrible creatures were still a terror and a credible threat, no matter one's age. A few had been clever enough to cross the wall, and they had indeed run amuck. One even dared to steal King Theron's Wayfinder berry. Luckily, the silly human girl was apprehended before she could glean the berry's power. Still, it scared her to pieces at what the human might have done had she obtained the berry. Why, she might have enslaved them all!

"Hobart!" she softly called into the night. "Here, little, sickly, green heathen!"

She despised trolls, for she found their lack of hygiene utterly repulsive. Their euphoric take on the world was adorable, however. They found joy in the most mundane items. Adding a wolf's head to a dragon doll's body or playing with something discarded, trolls were the epitome of euphoric happiness, doing whatever task their heart set upon. But their uncleanliness was also enough for her to remain far away from them. Known for popping snot bubbles and breaking wind enough to vanquish wee insects, she found them deplorable up close. *Always better from a distance,* she thought, grinning as she peered down an alleyway.

Faetilda shuddered as a burst of cold air caressed her cheeks. "Huckledew! Hartarlou! Where in blazes are you?"

Nimbly, she made her way down the cobblestone streets; the crunch of ice underfoot was her only companion as dawn was almost upon her. She turned to the left, trudging her way down the snow-speckled footpaths. A glimmering light from a large window cast its glow onto the street and caught her attention. It was the sole light flickering in any of the establishments.

"Herrowdil?" her soft voice called.

The door to a shoppe tentatively opened. A stumpy, green head emerged, waving a knobby-fingered hand in her direction. The guttural noises made her insides scream with delight that she had found them. Smiling broadly, she rushed over to her unruly charge. Herrowdil held the door open wider for her, allowing her entrance. She strode quickly through the establishment and straight to where the sounds of mayhem bumped and banged. Drawing the curtain aside enough to slip past, she observed the scene.

Five other little beasties, orbs lit with mirth, turned their attention her way. Faetilda's eyes took in what they had built. The makeshift toys were original troll creations with mismatched bodies and drab colors. Looking around the room, her eyes widened at the damage done to whomever the poor shoppekeeper happened to be. Tools of the trade had been scattered around. Supplies had been plundered, and some bottles were overturned to drip goo onto the table's surface. Her shoulders dropped. It was one thing to fear mortals; it was another to take their livelihoods and dash them into oblivion. Digging in her pocket, she fidgeted for coins and found her funds lacking. *She reasoned with a frown that they probably don't even have the same currency.*

"Huckledew," she began cautiously approaching the nearest troll.

"Hartarlou," it giggled as it shook its head at her.

"Oh... Right," Faetilda smiled, not really able to tell any of them apart. "It's time we depart from here before *the humans* wake up."

"Humans!" the trolls yelled as one.

Their little bodies leaped from the table as they screamed at the top of their lungs. Hobart, or perhaps Hollokow, knocked toys upon toys off of shelves. A jar of white something splattered all over the wooden floorboards. What she could only assume was hair used for dolls erupted out of the jar, floating all over and sticking to the pasty substance. Faetilda scurried to each beastie, trying to shush them as she flapped her hands at them; her attempts only made them bellow louder.

"Silence, or you'll wake them, and they'll eat us for breakfast!"

All the screaming ceased immediately as they stared at each other, tendrils of drool hanging from their opened mouths. Spying a burlap sack in the corner and moving to steal it, she returned to the trolls, shoving their wiggling bodies inside. For there was absolutely no way she could keep an eye on each one, let alone carry them individually over the wall. Thank the Creator for her fae strength in situations like these!

Her impeccable hearing picked up noises from above the stairs. Shoving Hartalou, the last troll, inside the scratchy sack, she darted out the door, mindful to close it softly. Peering cautiously all around her, Faetilda dashed for the wall, promising herself to come back tomorrow evening. This was her fault—the shoppekeeper's wares were ruined—and, by the Creator, she was going to make it right—even if it put her in danger.

Chapter Three

Unmerry Morning

Edmund opened his eyes as the faint light of dawn crept under the damask curtain of his bedchamber, and he groggily rose from the bed. He wiped the sleep from his bleary eyes, shoving his feet into a pair of dark house slippers. With a rush of alarm, his body set to shaking as the events from last evening swirled in his mind. All of his beautiful budding creations were ruined, and he was in very dire straits. Best to begin the day and see what could be salvaged if, indeed, it had been reality and not some horrible nightmare. He didn't care to ease his hunger. Bile threatened his sour stomach, churning in his core. Washing from the basin and shaving his face helped to calm his racing heart. By the time he was dressed all in black, he found his way down the staircase. He breathed in and out and in and out. There was no need to draw aside the curtain to his workroom. It hung limply from the rod like a downtrodden leaf barely hanging onto its branch. When had that happened?

Shuffling forward, unbidden tears glazed Edmund's eyes as he took in the colossal disaster that was his workroom. Paint splatters marred his dark walls and the wooden boards of the floor. Tufts of doll hair and fur meant to be used as trim on wintertide dresses were strewn about, stuck in puddles of milky glue. Hulking masses of wax were melted to create small hills of gunk atop his worktable. Distorted fingerprints left along the edges of the table were a reminder of the horrid creatures that had wrecked his life. Stepping further into the room, Edmund peered down toward the table to better see the creations in the early morning light that filtered through the small lead-paned window behind him. It was even more terrible than he had concluded just a few hours before, almost as if the beasts had returned. Had they?

Carved dragon heads, pointed teeth, snarling wolves, beings with elongated horns, and hoofed feet had been made from his most expensive wood stock. The delicate porcelain doll pieces were oddly affixed to bodies and no longer pale and lovely; they were now tawdry and ugly. There was more to catalog, but his heart, which felt battered and bloody, simply could not bear to see it. A single tear trickled from the corner of his gray eye and landed upon the cruel smile of a winged creature.

He didn't have another lifetime to recoup from this. Even if Edmund was a younger gentleman, this would still be crushing to his spirits and detrimental to his pocket; as would be for anyone. Why had he named his shoppe *Faerie Wishes*? Perchance, this was his due for using such a whimsical name and courting faerie antics. Was the epithet to blame? Had his business been chosen because of it? Shaking his dark head, he turned and walked toward the side of the room. A stack of empty crates stood awaiting customers' requests for his wonderful creations, such as a beautiful doll or a toy train, but those toys would now exist only in his imagination. He gingerly picked up the first crate and returned to the table. He began discarding the ruined playthings into the crate one after another and tried not to flinch as each one knocked against the other. As his mind calculated the cost of each piece, it couldn't be helped. When the task was finished, he strode to the back door of his shoppe, which was again unsecured. He walked through the doorway toward the communal pile of rubbish and deposited the crate there. A puff of cloud made from his breath rose before him as a shiver ran down his spine with spindly fingers. Edmund made his way back inside and repeated the process. When all the pieces were discarded, he picked up his broom and swept the litter from the floor. Next, it was quite an endeavor to clean the substances from the room's walls and surfaces, and some blemishes refused to be wiped away. The worktable would forever be stained, but that was the least of his worries.

Rumbles came from his stomach at half past ten, and Edmund nibbled on crackers and canned preserves and sipped from a bracing cup of tea. Having not yet ventured into his shoppefront, he had no idea what awaited him there. It took all of his mental strength to screw up his courage, but after satiating his hunger, Edmund breezed into the open area.

A shock, as if being doused in cold water, robbed the breath from his lungs as his heart struggled to beat. Globs of paint blemished his hanging puppets and clung to his wooden creations; the rocking horses, the dollhouses, and even the tin soldiers bore globs. His toy shoppe was a battlefield with fallen toys torn from shelves and stomped upon. The stuffing was ripped from furred bodies and draped everywhere. His mouth hung open, his eyes wild as they continued to scan the scene.

A harsh-sounding knock landed on the glass window of the shoppe's front door, rattling it and Edmund's nerves. Whirling around to face the entrance, the color fled from his cheeks. The dark glower of Lord Darlington stared at him. *Not now!* He wanted to fall to his knees and beg the man to go away.

Lord Darlington's face further darkened as Edmund stayed rooted to the spot. Could he ignore the man? Was it possible to ask the Creator to take him into his loving arms now? Edmund had lived a rich life, had he not? True, he had missed out on marriage and a family of his own, but he had found joy nonetheless. He had never longed to be whisked away to Faerie quite so much before. *Faerie Wishes*, indeed. If ever they were real, he needed their power right about now.

Shaking himself, he let his hands open and close to restore feeling to his arms. With trepidation, he crossed the space and unlocked the door. Pulling it open, he bowed his head before His Lordship.

"What an honor to receive you, my lord," he began as he straightened.

Surveying the disaster behind Edmund, His Lordship spoke. "Have ruffians attacked your shoppe? Why are the constables not here?" His dark brows knit together.

Wringing his hands together, Edmund replied, "I don't think they nor even the Bow Street Runners can be of help in this instance. It was a matter of *trolls...*"

"I say! Trolls? Here in our city?" His Lordship's lips curled with distaste.

Edmund nodded.

"I am not an unreasonable man. But is it possible that you have finished the dollhouse for my Adeline?"

"I had it nearly completed..." Edmund trailed off as he rubbed his jaw.

"And the trolls have dismantled it? Destroyed it?"

"Aye, that they have."

"Very well. In that case, I shall require my deposit back so that I may purchase another one from some other toymaker." Lord Darlington held out his gloved hand and wiggled his outstretched fingers.

"You are owed the funds, however—" Edmund paused, looking down at his booted feet.

"Surely you can come up with it."

"I just need a day or possibly two. To see what I can salvage and sell." Edmund lifted his gaze. The man was looking at Edmund as if he were an unwanted speck of dust clinging to his greatcoat.

Harrumphing, the English peer, stared down his nose at Edmund. "See that you do, good sir. Debtors' prison can be unsurvivable in wintertide. It's the bite of cold, you know. Carries the unsavory to their graves." With that, the gentleman swiveled on his heel and strode from the doorway into the bustling street.

Edmund closed the door and slumped back against it. If only he had a magical timepiece, he could use to restore time back to before all the chaos of the night took place. He'd clobber all the beasties over their ugly heads, no matter their unbridled joy. He was ruined, and the only avenue of survival was an escape. He loathed the idea of leaving his responsibilities to the wayside, but this was not his fault. He didn't set out to deceive anyone. Edmund's heart pricked at the thought of his good name being sullied, and scarlet shame colored his face at the idea he would disappoint any child, now or ever.

Chapter Four

Dashing All the Way

Faetilda's heart beat erratically in her chest. To cross The Wall once was scary enough, but to do it again, well, she felt idiotic. This was insane, absolutely ridiculous! But she simply had to. She owed it to the shoppekeeper to correct her wrongdoing. It was her fault the trolls had escaped and ransacked his business. Faetilda was the one who forgot to bolt the door. She forgot to lock the windows. She had taken her eyes from them for ten measly minutes to make them supper, and chaos had ensued.

Her fingers dipped into the pocket sewn into her empire-waisted dress, checking the golden coins, ensuring the proper amount was inside. Faetilda even considered wearing her jeweled necklace in case she required a more appropriate bargaining chip. Taking a deep breath, she climbed The Wall, remembering the best places to fit her fingers and the toes of her boots. Her arms didn't ache as terribly as they had yesterday from carrying those burdensome imps, so this climb was surprisingly better. Her muscles seemed steadier; perhaps the exercise had done her good.

Once at the top, Faetilda cautiously peered both ways before beginning the descent. Her insides roiled with fear. Yesterday, it was fear for the charges in her care, of them coming into contact with the horrid humans. This evening, it was fear of herself being imprisoned by one. She didn't tell Flora where she was going; she simply slipped away. In fact, she told no one about yesterday, for she was far too embarrassed. She could trust the trolls to remain mute, too busy with smashing and running amuck to recall what they had been about.

Worrying her lip between her teeth, she safely made it to the slushy ground. Faetilda dashed her way through the snowy streets, recalling the same path she'd taken last eve. She turned left, staring methodically at each building to be certain she was headed in the right direction.

She stopped and tilted her head to the side, wiping her red tendrils of hair from her eyes. The elegant white scroll on the window caught her attention. *Faerie Wishes*, she mused. *How odd. I missed this before. Perhaps the proprietor held a bit of whimsy in their heart?*

Faetilda felt lighter as she grasped onto the doorknob and twisted it. She bashed into the door, not expecting it to be locked. She had no need to ever lock her doors at home, but then she really had nothing of worth to steal. Huffing, she held her hand above the knob and willed what pool of magic she could still call upon to open the door. The lock instantly obeyed, and the tumblers turned, earning her triumphant smile.

Faetilda entered the shoppe, peering around. The room was softly lit by low light from the fireplace, and a glimmer of moonlight bouncing off the glittery snow outside streamed through the large windows. The poor shoppekeeper had tidied the best they possibly could. It must have taken them the better part of the day and a mountain full of patience to see to the monumental task. If only they had the aid of magic, it would've been a breeze. The makeshift dolls the trolls made were no longer in sight. Even the charming toys from the window were gone. No puppets hung from strings; the dollhouse and everything else had all been removed. To the rubble pile?

Faetilda frowned. *The poor dear. This is all my fault.*

She pivoted around in a slow circle, taking in the quaintness of the empty shoppe. A scream erupted as her eyes landed upon a strange man in a woman's dress, and she was surprised to realize she was the one who screamed. Without thinking it through, she strode up to the man who gaped at her and poked him in the cheek.

"Ugh," she blinked, poking it again. "It's so real."

The man let out a blood-curdling scream. Faetilda leaped away as another yelp escaped her. She stumbled, falling backward into a vacant shelf, and soundly smashed her elbows. The breath left her body as she struggled to weather the shooting pain from her elbows to her stomach. Grumbling once she could draw in air, she righted herself, dusting off invisible debris.

"Get out of my shoppe at once, you evil faerie!" The man snarled; his face paled.

"I'm not evil," she rebuked in a wounded tone. Why did humans think fae were evil when they were the ones who provoked fear?

"All fae lie. It's in your wicked nature!"

"I could say the same for you," she seethed, crossing her arms and fluttering her gossamer wings. "I came here only to help the person who made the toys those abominable trolls ruined."

The man crossed his arms over his chest, mirroring her pose. "How can I be certain you're not lying?"

"I can turn you into a newt and go about my business if that makes you feel any better."

"You can do that?" He paled even more.

"Are you willing to find out? I may very well be lying since you believe I'm something evil and wicked. But at least I'm not wearing the ugliest dress to ever exist."

"It's a nightgown," he retorted with indignation puffing up his chest.

Faetilda shrugged one shoulder. "Do you want my help or not?" This was growing tedious, and she wanted to be over The Wall again as soon as possible.

"What can you possibly do?" the man said, continuing to scowl at her.

Taking a step back, she looked at him fully. Dark hair was peppered with flecks of white and silver at the edges, just enough to lend him a distinguished air. Suspicious slate-gray eyes narrowed on her, taking stock of her every movement. The man was at least a head taller than her, perhaps more. Large hands bore scars on the back, no doubt from a troublesome mortal life. But he was terribly handsome for a human. The kind of handsome that got faeries into trouble...

"Open your mouth," she suddenly instructed.

"Whatever are you going to do?"

"See if you have pointy teeth."

The man guffawed. "And what if I do?"

"Well," she paused. "Does it hurt when you bite your tongue?"

"I don't have pointy teeth." He looked at her as if she had grown a pair of horns or maybe even a tail.

Faetilda nodded, satisfied he wasn't going to tackle her and munch on her bones. Swiveling around, she padded through the shoppe and through the curtained workroom to a halt before the work table. "Down to business then. What can I do to make this unfortunate event up to you?"

The man chuckled, swiping both hands over his face. "There's naught you can do. I'm ruined."

"Nonsense. I noted last evening that you had begun to fashion something from a lovely piece of ebony wood," she said, drawing her magic to her.

Silver mist enveloped her hands. She willed with her heart for neat stacks of ebony wood to appear atop the table. In a sparkling whoosh, five large pieces appeared.

The man's mouth popped open. She leaned toward him, pushing his chin up and closing his mouth.

"I don't know if you know this, but that's rather rude," she whispered, giving him a wink of her amethyst eye. Perhaps this mortal wasn't one to be frightened of after all. An endearing quality about him made her want to stay awhile by his side.

Chapter Five

All I Want for Christmastide

Was he dreaming this time? A rose-gold-winged faerie was flirting with him? True, she was magnificent, with the fiery tresses that endlessly framed her oval face and her amethyst eyes, which seemed to see right through him. Were all fae this ethereal? This beautiful? No wonder mortal men were cautioned never to cross The Wall.

A man could willingly go to his death to bask in their radiance. And when she had touched his chin with her tapered fingers, his heart had stalled. He was much too old to let fancy carry him off. Besides, he wasn't the man who turned female heads his way.

If Edmund had been asked this morning what he wanted most for Christmastide, he would have said he needed more stacks of the ebony wood to fulfill Lord Darlington's request. Was this stunning creature before him his Faerie Godmother? His stomach sank as a wave of sadness gripped him. It wasn't enough. The wood was wonderful, but his ruined tools, the other materials he needed to complete the dollhouse, he didn't possess any longer.

"Helloooo," she said, "Are you all right?"

Edmund nodded his head. "Quite. Thank you."

Her eyes pinched as her shoulders moved forward. "Is there anything else you need? Oh, I know!"

Her jubilant grin caused his heartbeat to hammer in his chest. Her smile was even more radiant, lighting up her entire face and making her even more ethereal.

"Where are your creations? Perhaps I might be able to salvage them?"

The offer made all the hope swell in his chest as he dared to believe her. "Surely, you jest?"

The faerie shook her head. "I do not. My magic is limited compared to others, but setting wrongs to rights is doable."

"You're welcome to try," he said, taking her through his shoppe and exiting through the back door to the cluttered rubbish pile that held the discarded toys, which were now under a fair amount of freshly fallen snow.

It nearly killed him to see all these ruined creations in this state, appearing as if they dwelled in a forgotten grave. To Edmund, it felt as though a pick had chipped away hunks of his heart. But he could do nothing now to undo what those blasted little heathens had done or recreate the toys, and brushing the snow from them would only be a fruitless effort.

The faerie beside him clucked her tongue as she scanned the mess. "Oh, my stars. Those horrid little imps," she said, shaking her head. Fiery red curls bounced and framed her face. "Here we go."

Silver magic pooled like water into her hand. Like a wish, she blew her magic out onto the snow-laden rubble pile of playthings. Edmund stared wide-eyed as the snow rose into the air and dissipated, and one by one, his creations were lifted into the air. Blobs of paint and sticky glue melted away. The ruined and twisted strings on his puppets realigned and became whole as their clothing rematerialized before his stunned eyes. His porcelain dolls glowed with their peaches and cream complexions instead of thick coats of ick, their correct parts reattaching to make themselves like new. This fabulous faerie had redone months of hard work in just seconds, giving him back his good name, his independence, and his belief in the good outweighing the bad. Again, his mouth dropped open.

"You must stop making that doddering face as if your wits have gone begging," the fae lady scolded. "It detracts from your handsome features."

"You've rescued me!" Edmund exclaimed, picking up a wooden girl puppet. "Thank you! Oh, thank you, thank you ever so much."

Faetilda covered her ears. "I've heard humans use pleasantries but never thought I would be on the receiving end. It is a rather barbaric custom, and I'd be *pleased* if you'd never do that again!"

Edmund dipped his head toward her apologetically before carefully settling the puppet back down amongst its fellows. Lifting one of the crates from the snow, he carried the cumbersome thing back through to the shoppe and straight to the center of his establishment. He was tickled; he was light as a feather! Edmund returned all his creations to rights, just as the gentle-faerie promised. His tools were an entirely other matter, but this was still far more than he thought to receive. Purchasing more tools would be easily achieved if he had sellable goods. Behind him, the other crates floated in the air along swirling mists of silver magic. Smiling, his rescuer waved her hand, and the crates lowered onto the wooden boards beside the other.

"What is this?" the faerie asked after a moment, pointing to the edge of the room. Edmund hadn't been able to toss it out, not while he was in such despairing spirits.

"It was once a dollhouse."

She laughed, and her melodic voice made his knees wobble, and goosebumps rose along his skin. Had he ever met someone more wonderful? Nay, indeed, he had not, human or otherwise.

"It's a wee house for sprites yet it is used for dolls?"

"What's a sprite?"

"Darling little things," she said, making motions with her hands to give the size. "They are so kind, sometimes bossy and bothersome, but all in good nature. Oh, but it's ruined, too," she sighed dejectedly. "Blast those little beasties!"

Edmund paused to watch her use the magic just as she had the last time. By all, it was an incredible feat! Even more so to see within swirling silver tendrils, the wooden picket fence surrounding the house become unbroken, and the furniture he had delicately made to become fused back together.

"I hope sprites are better received than trolls."

"Oh, by far, to be sure!" she said, carrying a puppet in her hands. "Well, let's not dawdle. I want to be back over The Wall by sunrise."

"What happens at sunrise?" Edmund asked, hanging the puppets from their appropriate hooks along the ceiling beam.

"Why, more humans come out," she said, blinking. "I don't wish to be eaten."

Edmund laughed. "We don't eat faeries."

"Oh," the lady fae beamed. "You're certain? Our limbs are not served in questionable pubs? Or our blood used when toasting the New Year?"

His face twisted in horror as he shuddered. Those ideas were disgusting. No wonder she was in a hurry to rush away; he'd be too. But did that mean if there were falsehoods about his customs, the same could be said for Faerie?

"Never! We are not quite that savage," he reassured her.

"Thank the Creator!" She clapped her hands together as she wiggled in a little dance.

Edmund caught himself grinning at her. The petite faerie stilled and pushed her hair behind her ear as she studiously watched him over long, dark lashes. Her creamy skin shimmered in the moonlight, but was that a slight blush coloring her cheeks?

"Well, it's been an absolute pleasure helping you. I must be getting back," she said, casting her eyes to the floor.

Edmund went to the cloak stand by the door, shrugging his own greatcoat on and wrapping a thick cloak around her.

"I'd be honored to escort you, fair lady," he said as the pair entered into the night.

Chapter Six

Faerie, It's Cold Outside

Faetilda grinned as the man kindly walked beside her back to The Wall, even going as far as covering her wings with a burgundy cloak so that she wouldn't be seen by more mortals who might not be so gallant. It might be true humans didn't eat fae, but nothing stopped them from capturing them in hopes of making their dreams come true. There were some *"collectors"* who coveted her kind, locking them away behind glass to waste away.

The blowing wind bit at their exposed skin as snowflakes landed upon banks of shoveled snow. The cobblestone street was slick in patches where black ice formed as the temperature plummeted.

"My goodness, it's freezing." Faetilda shivered as she began to lose the feeling in her fingertips. Her words hung in the air like a thick fog that lessened with each breath she took.

"It is. This Christmastide promises to be one of the coldest in years. I anticipate the sleds I sold these past weeks will be seen in abundance." His face lit with the happy thought as a puff of steam from his spoken statement disappeared into the atmosphere.

Faetilda's cheeks turned rosy as she watched how delighted this mortal man became in knowing his creations were well received. She turned her head to the right, avoiding his observant gaze. Before them, mist danced across the ground. They had reached The Wall. Faetilda shrugged from the cloak and handed it back to the toymaker. Her brows furrowed as she wondered what his name might be for the millionth time in the last few hours. She'd never heard that mortal names possessed power like fae names did. Faetilda had not been the name her mother had whispered into her pointed ear at birth. The name Faetilda had been gifted to her when the first visitor bestowed the baby with a kiss. The name had floated along the air in a quiet murmur resting in each faerie's ear, and so, she became Faetilda.

Tucking the cloak under his arm, the man's eyes pinched together as he posed the question, "Would it be impertinent to ask what your name is? So I may have it to remember you by?"

Her heart skipped a beat and leaped in her chest two more times as the rosy hue of her skin deepened. "Faetilda."

"That is beautiful. Do all faeries possess 'Fae' in their moniker?"

"No, that is not so. But our names are chosen for us by the Creator, and that was the address given to me." Her lips curved into a demure smile. "Am I to know yours?"

"Oh, of course." He reached for her hand and bowed before her. "Edmund Smithe, at your service." A warmth began in Faetilda's fingertips and spread straight to her heart.

"How dashing you are, sir," she replied as she dipped into a curtsy. Straightening, a crater of disappointment crept into her center, creating a sinking sensation in her stomach. Could she keep him? Possibly lure him over The Wall? It wasn't uncommon for some fae to abscond with willing mortals. Faetilda's heart didn't want to let him go, but she wasn't a robber of people and couldn't live with herself if she employed trickery to aid her cause. Let him go, she must, even if it was a colossal mistake to do so. What in all the realms was wrong with her?

"I hope that—" he paused, looking as if he was at a loss for words. Shrugging his shoulders, he smiled at her, but the smile lacked warmth and didn't reach his expressive eyes. Disappointment shadowed his features as he pushed the snow around with his booted foot, but quickly faded away when he looked back up at her. *What was that lingering in his gaze?*

"I hope your business flourishes and all your dreams come true," she told him with a slight wobble upon her lips.

Then she reached up, latching onto a stone, and she began to heft herself up toward the lip of the wall. With every inch, it was as if a flame burned another piece of her heart away. She couldn't explain it. Reaching the top of the fortification, she threw one leg over the edge and straddled the separator of their two worlds. Faetilda knew she shouldn't look down, not at Edmund. But she could no more stop her eyes from seeking him out than she could stop the beating of her heart.

Edmund's head was tilted up as he observed her. His breaths escaped in tendrils of steam. Lifting his hand, he waved at her, and mist gathered in her eyes. Returning his wave, she made herself break their stare and let her other leg descend to the side of Faerie, calling her home.

Edmund stood in front of The Wall until his fingers went completely numb, and his eyes stung from the biting winter chill. He had to be absolutely certain she was gone. Or was his heart hoping she would come back?

Rubbing the aching area over his heart, he kept vigil until the wisps of fiery red tresses disappeared completely. Why did he long to traverse the structure and rush headlong into Faerie? Was he mad? Or in the grips of some enchantment that, by being in her presence, had altered his thoughts? Edmund didn't believe she had done anything to him, hadn't placed a hex of some sort upon him. Faetilda wasn't that sort of creature. His heart, as well as his mind, told him this was so. She didn't have to come back to repair the damage. Yet, she had. And left more wreckage in her wake if the painful beating of his heart was an accurate measure. It was time to return to his home, to quell his restless heart and mind, and to finally indulge in a good night's sleep. After all, he wasn't some young buck who could cavort across all of Britain, ushering in dawn's first light.

Taking care of his steps so he didn't injure himself with a fall, Edmund picked his way back through the streets with the gentle glow of the street lights. It seemed as if he arrived at his shoppe in no time, so lost in his thoughts. Withdrawing his brass key and fitting it into the lock of his front door, he twisted the knob and pushed his way inside. He blinked his eyes and then blinked again just to be sure his establishment was indeed how they'd left it; everything was in its proper place and in perfect condition.

Striding over to his worktable, Edmund picked up a porcelain doll, turning it over in his hands. He had yet to put hair upon its alabaster head. *How magnificent would she look with red hair and lovely amethyst eyes?* he thought. He gently laid the doll down, turning upon his heel. He could make a hundred dolls, and nothing would be akin to her likeness in beauty.

Trudging up his staircase, Edmund walked into his bedchamber and gingerly sat down in the sole chair it possessed. After discarding his greatcoat, tailcoat, and cravat onto the end table near him, he then leaned forward to remove his Hessian boots. All the while, a graceful smile and the flutter of rose-gold wings waltzed across his vision. Faetilda was all he could see, all he wanted to see, and he would never get to see her again.

"Edmund was quite dazzling for a mortal," Faetilda dreamily confessed to her friend, Flora, who looked at her with a frown, marring her ebony complexion.

"Yes, dearie. You keep saying the exact same thing. Should you not let thoughts of him wither away now that this entire business is behind you?" Flora perked a golden brow as her eyes filled with sympathy.

"You are right," Faetilda sighed as a brittle smile curved her lips. "I know you are. If only I could. There is something about him that calls to my soul."

Flora gasped, "You don't mean to say you believe he's your Fated Mate?"

Faetilda fluttered her lips in an unladylike manner, for the notion sounded preposterous. "How could that be? What a ridiculous notion."

"Indeed, and yet, have we not witnessed it with our own eyes in the king's retinue, no less! That dashing guard returned with his Fated Mate, and she was lovely. It's not an impossibility..." Flora trailed off as her eyes scanned the horizon, lost in thought.

"He would not view this world as we might. I could not drag him here and hope he loves Faerie as much as I do. Plus, *Faerie Wishes* is his life, his absolute preoccupation—"

"Yet he named his shoppe after Faerie! Doesn't that sway your opinion, even the tiniest amount? His soul knows you, even if his mind hasn't quite caught up to the fact. You should visit him again this evening! Discover what lies between you." Flora's golden curls bobbed along her shoulder as she nodded her head.

"Not every faerie is meant to be as happy as you and Finnius are," Faetilda retorted.

"Nonsense and rubbish! Go to him. You needn't fall instantly in love with the man, but you must suss out what lingers betwixt you two."

Faetilda wanted to argue, to have the good sense to be critical and think this through. But the passing three nights hadn't allowed her to distance herself from the specter that haunted her dreams and prodded her heart in her waking hours. She felt haunted by him, and though she had never been lonely before, the hollow ache of the emotion ate at her insides with savage, pointed teeth.

She hadn't been able to find joy in her duties, even though being a tooth-faerie had always set her spirits soaring. Faetilda adored visiting faerielings and collecting their teeth. Leaving a sachet of sweet treats by their bedside had always filled her with glee. She was a happy faerie and since meeting and leaving that man, she hadn't truly smiled with genuine affection. In short, she was not herself, and she hadn't any idea how to reclaim her cheerful sentiments. Perchance, another visit wouldn't be amiss.

"Very well, I shall take your advice and visit him tonight. But what if—" her brows kissed as she attempted to ponder all of the ways this could go horribly wrong. Just because Edmund was a wonderful human and hadn't hurt her, it didn't mean she was safe in his world.

"But what if?" her friend prompted her with a wave of her hand.

"He might not want me. How embarrassing to suffer some silly faerie crush if it's all for naught."

Leaning forward over the tabletop separating them, Flora spoke with determination. "Go get your human and see where fate leads you next!"

"I shall," Faetilda decided on a rush of adrenaline, and her breath labored under her rioting feelings. She would do this, and if there was a chance they were each other's happily-ever-afters, then that story would begin tonight.

Chapter Seven

Oh, Come All Ye Beasties

Rap, tap, thump!

"Oh no!" Edmund sprung from his bed as his heart raced and sweat broke out on his forehead. The trolls were back! He wouldn't let the beasties destroy his work again! Shoving his feet into his slippers and reaching for his dressing gown that lay atop the foot of his bed, he stomped his way down the staircase and straight past his workroom to the center of his shoppe.

The moonlight was bright as it glowed, drawing his eyes upon the creatures standing around and gaping at him. Indeed, the trolls had returned, and they wore jagged-toothed smiles as they watched him. Pivoting his focus away from the ghastly beings, he nearly shouted with fright as a massive male fae with antlers and hulking muscles unwaveringly met his stare. Edmund's mouth went dry as his hopes plummeted. If the being wanted to smash his way through the shoppe, there was nothing Edmund could do to stop him.

"You must be Edmund?" came a musical voice.

He had to use all of his willpower to look away from the frightening faerie and to the owner of the voice. A beautiful, ebony-skinned fae stood beside the male with a timid smile upon her features.

"Y-y-yes," he stuttered.

"Oh, how lovely. Tell me, do you have our dearie Faetilda locked away somewhere?" inquired the golden-haired beauty.

"No, of course not!" Ice filled his heart and impeded his heartbeat. "Is she missing?"

"She is. And it's been two nights since I parted from her. I was hopeful that tonight I'd see her wings carrying her safely back." The female fae swallowed as tears glimmered in her golden eyes.

"It's been five nights since she left here. I saw her over The Wall myself." Edmund took a small step toward her, and the hulking male growled. The hair on Edmund's neck and arms rose as fear spiked in his core.

"Behave yourself, Finnius!" she chided with a *tsk* of her tongue. "He won't harm us." Looking from the brute to Edmund again, she asked, "You won't, right?"

"Nay."

"Alright then, we must make a plan. A rescue. Finnius is an excellent tracker, he can locate Faetilda for us."

"What about the beasts?" Edmund motioned to the trolls, inching closer to his workroom curtain. One was studiously shoving his finger up his nose as he clomped along. Edmund's lip pulled into a grimace. He didn't want to view what, if anything, the troll would reveal on its fingertip.

"Little Ones, mind yourselves. Now is not the time to run amuck!" she scolded the trolls, who moved to stand at her side again, grumbling as they complied.

Pinching the bridge of his nose, the antler-faed male grunted. "I told you to leave them in Faerie."

"Not happening. They are my charges, and you vowed to put up with them, no matter what!" the golden-haired faerie admonished.

"So I did," Finnius admitted with a deep sigh.

"Now we just need a bit of magic and to have you aid us, and we shall be prepared for anything." Her eyes roved over the toys and came to rest on the tin soldiers. "Yes, you shall do, my little fellows!" Withdrawing a golden wand from her cloak, the faerie waved her wand, and it began to glow while golden stars danced from its tip. Casting the shining heavenly bodies over to the soldiers, the toys began to glimmer and were lifted into the air. Each soldier grew in size until they were taller than Edmund. Then, moving as one, they all landed on the floor before him, saluting him as they towered over him, standing proud with their shoulders back, their keen eyes taking in everything around them.

"Well, address your army, Edmund, for they are yours to command!" the wand-wielding faerie prompted him.

Edmund's mouth gaped as he pointed to himself.

"General, we await your orders," said one of the soldiers stepping from formation. He was an exact copy of his comrades. They were garbed in red regimental coats, extended breeches, polished black boots, and carried swords with silver handles. Their bodies and clothing still retained a metallic quality and it amazed Edmund they could talk and move.

"Are we certain this is a good idea, Flora?" Finnius grouched out as his tan face looked skeptical.

"Of course I am! Time is of the essence. Even now, our friend could be forever parted from us, and I must know the reason why! What evil villain has taken her?" Flora stomped her foot as her eyes narrowed to slits.

Edmund eyed the creatures and shook himself. Trolls, faeries, and tin soldiers sprung to life in his toy shoppe; it defied the senses! Looking to Finnius, who seemed like a leader, made sense in the midst of this chaos.

Finnius felt Edmund's scrutiny as the faerie stood taller and folded his arms across his chest. "Right then, Flora, my love. I think it's best that I scout out the land and ascertain whether I can catch her scent. We can give orders once we know which direction we need to go." He met Edmund's stare and gave a slight nod of his head.

"Very well, let's hop to it. Daylight is our greatest foe, so let's make haste." Flora clapped her hands as she grabbed onto the nearest troll and steered it toward the exit.

"Do I have a moment to properly dress? It's freezing outside, and I am liable to catch my death otherwise." Edmund looked from the back of Flora to Finnius, who were already heading out of doors to see to his task.

"Oh, yes. But do hurry, mortal Edmund. We must make haste!" Flora canted her head back to see him.

Edmund pivoted on his slippered heel, and thunderous footsteps followed in his shadow. He halted abruptly and whirled back around, facing his troops. Lifting a hand, he stayed their momentum. "I require you to stay here and guard the shoppe until I return."

"As you command, General Mortal Edmund." His lieutenant saluted Edmund, his coal-colored eyes shining and bright. The other soldiers kept the line behind him.

"'Tis just Edmund or Mister Smithe," Edmund informed the eager faces as he turned and made his way up to his bedchamber. It took little time for him to don the appropriate clothing, and within minutes, he was striding from his locked shoppe and standing in the snow beside the visitors.

"I think we need to head north. I lost her scent fairly quickly, and so, I must conclude that she was placed into some conveyance to carry her away two nights ago," Finnius remarked. His scowl twisting his features and making his appearance more fearsome.

Something dark twisted inside Edmund as his heart cracked in half and his chest seized. Faetilda had come back to visit him just two evenings past, and he had no clue that just outside his business, she had been spirited away. Why had she ventured back?

"Right," Flora breathed out, interrupting his musings and latching onto her beau's arm. "Best to link arms so we leave no faerie, troll, human, or toy behind."

Edmund didn't want to touch the foul-smelling beasts, so he maneuvered himself beside his soldiers. They looked like rule followers, and, to his mind, those who followed the rules didn't tend to go against social cues.

Their party moved closely together under a twinkling sky blessedly free from clouds, seeking to dump snow upon their heads. He'd take the blessings where he may. Raising his gaze, Edmund silently sent a prayer into the ether. He couldn't fathom the idea that Faetilda had come to harm when he'd been completely ignorant of her disappearance. He felt as if he had failed her; magic aside, she was a stranger to this realm and there were evil men who captured the fae to entertain their guests and even to experiment upon the poor creatures. Buckingham House had even hosted a gathering last year, just after the new year, so that onlookers could gawk at the hostages in the safety of the queen's guards. Queen Charlotte was known to pay exorbitant sums to anyone who could enlarge her menagerie with differing residents of Faerie. He had made the mistake once in joining the festivities, and the broken faces and drooping wings he had observed were enough to bring shame upon him. He had no desire to meet with the fae before, but now, he was coming to find their kind much less frightening. He felt there was even a camaraderie forming amongst them.

We're coming for you, Faetilda. Just be strong until we rescue you. And we will *rescue you, I shan't be able to rest until we do.*

Chapter Eight

Silent Night

A renegade tear trekked down her face as Faetilda strained her pointed ears for any sign that her captor was returning to break the eerily silent night. The man was pure evil, boasting gluttonous green eyes and a dark, twisted smile that had sent icy fear racing through her veins. He was a human who didn't care for the value of life, and his cruel commands proved this.

When she scaled The Wall two nights ago in hopes of reaching Edmund to discover where his heart lay, her captor had lurked amongst the shadows before she had even crossed the street to Faerie Wishes. The abysmal man had surprised her, popping out of an establishment's recessed doorway. Slapping a cold and clammy hand around her mouth before she could even let out a scream, the other hand encircled her waist and crushed her delicate wings. Jolting shocks of fire lanced her back at the barbaric treatment as Faetilda fought with everything she had in her to break free, but it wasn't enough. Her magic, weak as it was even in Faerie, wasn't enough to pack much of a punch to get her assailant to relent. Her attacker removed his hand, and a dark sack reeking of stale ale and rotten food was wrenched over her head. She hadn't even had a moment to draw in breath or to cry out. More rough hands grabbed at her body, and her feet were lifted from under her as mortal men grumbled, tying rough rope around her wrists and ankles. Even now, sitting on a freezing floor in a darkened stone room, she sat bound and gagged. She had lost all feeling in her limbs days ago. She attempted to dip into her well of magic, but it was futile like it wasn't even there at all.

Faetilda bent forward, attempting to undo the ropes for the thousandth time in the last two days, even though the movement pulled at her wounded wings. Every so often, the horrible man would come to check on her, leer at her, then walk away, absent of his henchmen. He didn't have to say a word. She quite clearly saw the cruelty in his eyes, for they shimmered with malice. The two guards standing on the other side of the door boasted about their raises in pay for her capture and eventual turnover to Queen Charlotte. *The human queen!* The one who collected faeries as one might a bug, keeping them in glass enclosures and poking them with sharp-tipped instruments to see how they might react.

Faetilda tried her best not to think of that evil queen but to distance herself from her trepidation. But, her friends had disappeared over The Wall in search of their Fated Mates who might be dwelling amongst the mortals and never returned. Word eventually reached the residents of Faerie of the lost fae who had been taken prisoner behind the grande doors of the world-famous menagerie. A band of brave fae had vowed to rescue the friends but never returned. Now, she was to join those who were lost to Faerie. Guilt made her heart hurt as she thought about the dear friends she had left behind; the very last thing she desired was for them to worry or to mourn her loss and never know what her fate was.

A rumble shattered the dangerous atmosphere as her stomach gave Faetilda the not-so-gentle reminder she hadn't been properly filling it. She frowned as she tried to take deep breaths. There was nothing she could do about the hunger pangs. Her captor had thrown a bowl of some thick substance at her twice and stale bread once, but her eyesight caught the mold beginning to grow, and she discarded the unfit food by tossing them to the side of the small room. Faetilda had felt a measure of disobedience and a small thrill at her actions. Her empty belly, however, seemed not to appreciate the misbehavior.

The heavy metal door groaned on its hinges as it was shoved open, drawing her thoughts to the brutes before her.

"Grab the faerie," her captor bellowed. "Her Majesty sent word and payment for the horrid beast."

Scowling at her, he stepped aside, permitting two officers in scarlet tailcoats to enter the chamber. Faetilda nearly swooned with fright as her eyes widened and her nostrils flared. The vicious rumors she'd heard about the Queen's Men made her stomach churn, and bile rose to the back of her throat. They were the ones who carried out Queen Charlotte's deplorable orders. Even though they were bound to the wishes and dictates of their queen, Faetilda despised them all the same. What sorts of humans carried out such brutality? Their souls had to be corrupted. Not even her King Theron was this cruel.

Each guard bent toward Faetilda, grabbing her roughly by her upper arms and dragging her out of the cell. Her feet never even found purchase with the ground as she was carried up a flight of steps, through a massive entryway, and into the blustery night. The bitter cold made her nose sting and peppered her eyes. Tears slipped down her cheeks on their own accord, leaving frozen trails.

Awaiting them was a carriage with a matching pair of snow-white horses. There was also a black box encased in swirls and chains of iron. Even if she could get her hands free, her magic would be useless; she was already so drained. The solid black metal door swung outward. Her Majesty's men tossed Faetilda in like a rag doll; not even an ounce of care was given to her. Faetilda winced as she landed on her shoulder and struck the back of her head, seeing golden stars twirling before her eyes as her empty stomach continued churning. The door slammed behind her, reverberating, and making her wish for death instead of whatever was to become of her. She could handle death, to never dance under the stars of Faerie, to never bask in the rays of the rose gold sun... But to never have the chance to see Edmund and explore what might have been was utterly heartbreaking.

The carriage rocked forward, drawing an alarmed scream from Faetilda. Her pitiless cries were blocked by the gag in her mouth. The horses started out slowly, the clippity-clop of their hooves echoing against the cobblestone street. When the speed increased, it felt like they were zooming toward her final doom.

Although the plea felt selfish, Faetilda closed her eyes and wished someone would come to rescue her. Knowing Flora, her best friend, was already plotting a rescue when she didn't show back up. Faetilda wished she didn't. If these humans were so easily able to capture and subdue her and those before her, then who knows what they would do to her dearest and most treasured friend? It wasn't a fate she wished to share.

Faetilda kept her eyes closed and moved her body, tucking into the corner in the hopes of it helping to keep her from pitching to and fro during the awful ride that seemed to never end. Was she so hopeless that she longed for its conclusion, or did she never want the bruising bumps to cease?

Chapter Nine

Dancing Around the Christmastide Tree

Edmund restlessly twitched beside Finnius, ready to pounce on the officers who were roughly shoving Faetilda into a carriage with the queen's seal. What he had feared was coming to pass. Currently, he and his friends outnumbered the enemies. However, he was uncertain how many soldiers Lord Darlington harbored inside his townhouse walls; it wasn't possible to take them all on. Not only was that a particular issue, but more men were likely to hear the skirmish and come rushing from the houses on Mayfair Street where the elite of Society were sleeping. The very last thing they needed was more of the priggish peers to flee into the street brandishing weapons. His heart stilled in his chest at the muffled cry Faetilda made when she landed inside the conveyance. By goodness, the savages would pay! He'd personally see to it. He commanded his own band of warriors and would certainly use them to the advantage of the surrounding group.

When the carriage wheels clattered over the cobblestone street, Finnius held up his hand to signal they needed to wait and not run after it. They didn't need to keep the conveyance in their sights; they all knew where the carriage was taking their friend.

"We need more allies," mused Finnius as he stroked his dark beard.

"But where shall we find them?" asked Flora, twisting her ungloved hands together.

"Over the wall. Many faeries would fight for the chance to free their loved ones. It would be a Christmastide holiday never to be forgotten. But we mustn't tarry. We can use the daylight hours to recruit and gather weapons, then return come nightfall." With a determined nod, Finnius pivoted and began to jog at a brisk pace, retracing their steps toward Faerie Wishes. They had gone in a circuitous route, but now, he seemed to know which way The Wall lay. Perchance Faerie was calling to him?

The snow had long since turned his exposed face blue. Edmund could barely feel his limbs; his boots were a sodden mess, and his toes nothing more than sticks of ice. But he would carry on and follow Finnius, even if it meant his destination was over the dreaded wall.

Would he be safe? It didn't matter; his course was set. Their party reached the fortification in half the time the search had taken, and it was a good thing, too. The wispy fingers of dawn were creeping across the sky to steal the night away.

"Right, I guess it's my job to get the human over this thing." Finnius turned to Edmund and critically eyed him.

"He doesn't look terribly heavy," added Flora in a sweet tone with a hopeful note. It was clear they were all past frozen and weary.

Bending his knees, Finnius motioned to his back, "Just grab a hold, and whatever you do, don't let go."

Tentatively, at first, Edmund closed the distance between them. Feeling more emboldened, he placed one sure hand atop the faerie's shoulder and then the other as he let his legs wrap around the male's middle. A slight flush crept into his skin during the entire encounter. He was not a lad, and this was the most emasculating thing he had ever done. But there was nothing for it; he must comply to ensure this mission didn't fail.

Finnius agilely climbed The Wall as Edmund squeezed his eyes shut. On either side, the trolls rose up in the air, giggling their way to the top. The bright burst of Flora's golden magic was visible through his eyelids. He hoped that, with all his might, Finnius's strength would hold out. He didn't want to fall, and if the hulking male fell atop him, Edmund wouldn't survive. Below them, the clank of metal bodies hitting against stone let Edmund know his soldiers were following.

With a massive grunt, Finnius reached the very top of the structure. He took a moment to catch his breath, then speedily descended to Faerie.

"You can let go now, Mister Edmund," Flora chortled at him.

Peeling one eye open, then another, Edmund allowed his body to slip from Finnius. Straightening his greatcoat, he cleared his throat. Finnius turned around to scold one of the trolls, relieving himself on The Wall. Edmund quickly walked a few paces away to keep the liquid from his boots. He was in such an unsettled state that this didn't even phase him; he didn't crinkle his nose nor frown at the offending creature.

Before him was a winter wonderland. Huge mahogany tree branches held bundles of snow while the dawning day's horizon was glowing to life under a rose-gold sun. Twinkling teal stars were slowly fading from view; he couldn't wait to see their vibrancy come nighttime. In the distance, smoke rose with twisted tendrils, leaving Edmund to suspect homes dotted the scenery beyond the woods.

"You little bad troll, no more of that," admonished Flora as she bent down to drag the miscreant away by the tip of his green-pointed ear. "Form a line, wee ones," she directed the other trolls.

Edmund caught the eyes of his troops and motioned his head forward, letting his metal men know he wanted them to follow after Finnius, Flora, and their charges.

They traversed the forest floor where the snow was the thinnest, and they kept a straight path. Edmund's stomach gave a large growl and Finnius turned back to raise his bushy eyebrows at him. Edmund gave him a rueful smile in return. His stomach grumbled, twisting with pangs. He was starving and thought from the very vocal grunts and whines from the trolls he wasn't the only one. After they trekked for what seemed like another hour, the trees began to thin, giving a view of quaint little cottages with thatched roofs.

Snow-laden bird feeders and happy-faced faeries created from glittering snow stood in yards amongst the stepping stones. Faerielings rode sleds down a hill off to the side, their merry shouts and laughter filling the air.

A larger building stood before a rotunda with brick walls and a cream wooden door. Edmund followed the others, stomping the snow from his boots and crossing the threshold through the door. Continuing down a long corridor, they came to a stop in a large room with a high ceiling, which was lit with suspended teal faerie lights. A fireplace with a jolly blaze gave warmth, and he couldn't stem the sigh that passed his frozen lips. To feel the heat again after fearing your demise in the bitter cold of wintertide was a wonderful thing!

In the corner was a massive pine tree whose roots ran through the wooden floorboards. It was alight with the twinkling flames that must have been enchanted as the branches never caught fire. Bows in gold and silver gathered the light and mirrored it while tinier lights wove around the tree. Wee sprites? And were they dancing around the Christmastide tree? Pinecones and cinnamon twigs clung to its branches. Edmund had heard about the German tradition of bringing trees indoors to decorate and keep for the season. Did they get their idea from Faerie?

Pointing to the oblong wooden table with matching benches on either side, Flora ordered Edmund and the trolls to sit. The tin soldiers moved to the wall and stood straight at attention.

"Maggery, we've returned," Flora called as she came to stand behind each troll, unwinding the knitted scarves from each beast. She dropped them into a pile, then hurriedly deposited them onto a metal stand before the fire grate.

A purple-skinned lady faerie with shimmering skin, as if thousands of diamonds were embedded along her face and hands, floated into the dining room, carried by the large butterfly-shaped wings attached to her back. Her amethyst eyes landed on him, and her lips turned down to a frown.

"Oh no. You've brought one of those pesky humans back with you? What am I to do with it? Poke it with something?" Maggery's eyes widened when Edmund glared at her. "It seems to have a temper."

"Mister Edmund is our guest. I suspect," Flora began, then pranced over to Maggery and whispered into her pointed ear. The two looked at him as they spoke.

"Why all the secrecy?" huffed Finnius. "Do you really think he doesn't deserve to know? It's not as if after breaking into The Queen's House, he'll be welcomed to remain a free British citizen."

Canting his head to Finnius, Edmund asked, "What should I know? I already came to the conclusion I'd remain a prisoner of Her Majesty and charged with treason. I knew what my fate was to be the moment I decided to aid your cause." He swallowed to moisten his dry mouth. "And I have no regrets if we do, in fact, win the day; I shall meet my end with grace. Faetilda is worth the price."

"Aww, you see? It further proves the point!" Flora excitedly twirled in place.

"She means to say that Faetilda had an inkling you are her Fated Mate," explained Finnius, with impatience making his scowl look fiercer.

"Pardon me, but what's that you say? What in all the realms is a 'Fated Mate'?" Edmund extended his legs under the table; his joints were in agony now that feeling was returning to them. The joys of growing old were ever-present.

"Oh!" Flora's periwinkle wings fluttered as she flew to stand behind him, clapping her hands with glee. "Why, it's the most magical happening in Faerie. The most important thing to ever happen to one of fae lineage. Every being has a Fated Mate, even humans. However, your race just isn't magical enough to always find yours, and I think you call them 'soulmates'?"

Soulmates? That, he understood! The one meant for, and that was created for, just you alone. The other half of your soul is given by the Creator. And dear, precious Faetilda was crossing The Wall again to be with him because she felt the pull greater than he did? He rubbed a hand over his aching heart. True, he did feel an undeniable connection. Sitting still, he let his thoughts scatter like falling snowflakes waltzing along the heavens.

"You've broken him," Maggery said with a note of annoyance in her tone.

Edmund pulled the wool from his mind by shaking his head. "That's wonderful news. Does it mean I can return with her?"

"Of course it does, you silly man!" Flora told him. "Maggery, we're all quite famished, so let's spell together a meal and get to plotting. We have a dear faerie to rescue!"

"And the others, too," Finnius stated. "The queen will rue the day she caged our kin!"

"Cheers to that, Beloved," Flora grinned.

Edmund nodded, his mind churning with ideas of how to break into a fortified castle when others had failed.

Chapter Ten

Blue Wintertide

This wintertide was certain to be the saddest Faetilda had ever lived if she didn't first perish from some horrifying malady or torture. The mean-faced officers on either side of her escorted her through a stone-covered hallway. At the very end of the corridor, their grip tightened; cruel fingertips dug harshly into her arms. Their booted feet stomped to the right, carrying her further into the horrid queen's lair and descending a set of dark, dank stairs hidden behind a false wall.

Faetilda held her breath, not wanting to breathe another moment more. They entered through a lowly lit opening, and the pathway ahead looked bleak. The oppressive air of the tunnel made her vision swim, and her stomach clench. Double oak doors at the end were guarded on either side by a half dozen soldiers who didn't bat an eye at her presence. The doors swung outward at their approach. The Queen's Men stepped to the side, lips curling as if she were the most horrid creature in all the world. Faetilda let the breath whoosh from her lungs as she closed her eyes. If she had the power to grant wishes, she knew exactly what she'd wish for. The chance to escape and take all the poor creatures dwelling within along with her.

The officers carried her through the doors; her feet dragged along the floor behind her. Tortured gasps exploded through the ether, causing ringing in her ears. Faetilda tentatively glanced up as her heart forgot how to beat. Cages upon cages hung from rusted chains suspended from the ceilings. Glass domes covered pitiful beings who emulated dejection and sorrow. Her eyes took in each and every friend she had lost to the wickedness of the humans. The breath hitched in her lungs when her eyes landed on Jazmyne. The beautiful faerie had her hands pressed up to the glass dome that covered her; her once gorgeous and alluring purple butterfly wings were now both wilted and dulled.

Heads snapped in Faetilda's direction, dreadfully watching her progression toward an empty cage. Jazmyne shook her sunflower hair, tears streaming down her cheeks. Teardrops slipped from Faetilda's eyes, unbeknownst to her, as she was too numb to process her feelings when in the midst of such savagery. Faetilda hung her head, accepting no rescue attempt would ever be successful in freeing her.

Here, amongst at least two dozen other fae, she would remain for the rest of her days. The one guard holding her up on the right let go of her arm. Seizing her chance with a rush of adrenaline, Faetilda stomped on the toe of another soldier and sent her elbow flying behind her into the stomach of the officer.

Faetilda used what limited magic she had to create an orb, but she had to be careful. She was too far from The Wall to nurture the well her power resided in. The magic built slowly and bubbled in her hands. A black-haired Queen's Man gasped. The other cried for reinforcements, his shouts making the fae prisoners flinch. Faetilda launched the large orb, sending the men backward amid their curses and the sounds of their boots skittering to hold their places.

Whirling on her heel, Faetilda floundered to find purchase and run. The guards on the other side of the doors came bursting through the doorway. Faetilda used her very last reserves to cast her magic, making herself invisible to the eye. She usually only ever employed the spell on the unruly fae children when she tried to collect their teeth, but now was of the utmost urgency. The magic fizzled in her hands, sending her heart to her stomach with terror. The flame of her power had burned itself out.

"Run, Tilda!" Jazmyne screamed. "RUN!"

Faetilda darted around an officer lunging for her and just missed the tips of his meaty fingers. She dashed past numerous cages obstructing her path. Two guards blocked her route to escape out the double doors. The clambering of footsteps resounded from the hallway, coming ever closer.

Faetilda's heart thundered in her chest. She summoned a spark of what little magic remained, and it flickered to life, blasting the guard nearest her and sending him backward. Seizing her moment, she sprinted over him. The other officers grabbed her, catching her by the ankle. Faetilda fell to the hard stone ground, her elbows receiving a crushing blow that made bright stars shine across her vision. Gasping, she clambered back to her feet to bolt as soon as she could. Putting weight on her ankle caused her breath to gallop from her chest in misery. The ankle wasn't broken, just severely sprained. Were Faetilda in Faerie, she'd heal at a quicker pace or have access to a potion of healing.

Jazmyne screamed behind her, urging her to dart away as quickly as she could. A dozen guards rounded the corner, making their quick pursuit toward her. Faetilda gained her footing, begging her wings to work so that she might be able to fly; they were too cold, hardly offering her a flutter. But her best chance to flee was via her wings, and if she couldn't use them—

Officers from behind Faetilda appeared before she could move and forcefully seized her arms. One pinched her wings together like one might a wayward chicken. Faetilda screamed, arching her back to stem the fiery flow of lava that burned through her body. The excruciating torment sent Faetilda to her knees as she begged them to release her. Their bruising hands grabbed at her, subduing her to the ground, completely pinned.

She found her face pressed into the stone-cold floor, and the sticky fluid adhered to her skin and seeped into her fiery hair, coating her tear-stained cheeks. If this was to be her fate, she wasn't sure she could endure the carnality. But what choice did Faetilda have? They might have been easier on her had she not attempted to outrun them. Her conscience would not allow her to submit willingly, and that wasn't in her makeup.

Rough hands lifted her from the ground, carrying Faetilda back inside the horrid room housing her kin. The officers threw her into a lonely cell at the very back of the dungeon; her eyes struggled to take in its dimensions. Faetilda's back collided with the wall to the crunch of her wings, further mangling the pair. Faetilda howled in pain as she fought to suck in another breath with lungs that didn't want to function.

Slowly, she rose to her knees, begging her legs to hold her weight. She grabbed onto the black bars, hoisting herself up. She hissed from the biting cold of the metal and the hollow sickness spreading into her center. The guards laughed now that they had contained her, remarking on her feeble plight to escape.

Feeble? It had been noble!

Faetilda hung her head and allowed all the hurt and fear to spread to the marrow of her bones. More tears slipped from her eyes to the tip of her nose. She should never have left Faerie or crossed The Wall a third time. And as much as she wished she never had, having met Edmund made her soul alight in flames. Faetilda would never know whether he harbored any feelings for her in return. Her only Christmastide wish for the past several years was to find her Fated Mate, and even if she'd never spoken the thought aloud, it had lived in her heart. Now, for all the wintertides to come, her heart's desire would remain forever blue.

Chapter Eleven

The Caroling of the Bells

Edmund paced the lovely bedchamber, his mood sour in the atmosphere of such holiday cheer. His eyes alighted on the lace snowflakes clinging to the silk-papered walls, their intricate patterns drawing his eyes. His mechanical mind wanted to study them, as they put him in mind of the gears in his wind-up bears. From outside his window, the sounds of trolls and faerielings cavorting across the frozen landscape with shrieks of merriment and laughter ate at the hollowness of his soul and how he wanted to share the wonder of this realm with the one who made him dare to dream impossible dreams. Was it truly possible they had been created one for another?

After a riveting breakfast with Flora and Finnius and, of course, the trolls who slurped their gruel and gave him toothy smiles, he was allowed to retire to a small chamber. The four-postered bed and the downy pillows had been the softest that had ever cradled his wretched bones. However, sleep eluded him. He had tried to pace the hallways, but the hanging sprigs of holly berries and mistletoe swung with the movement of air every time his footfalls changed direction. Thoughts of Faetilda stuck in a horrid cage or, even worse, inside the deplorable queen's dungeon made any task impossible to bear. Every thought was of her. And every breath he took hurt when he didn't know if she was still living. It wasn't uncommon, surely, for the residents of the menagerie to be culled to make room for more. How long a lifespan did one have when incarcerated? His Faetilda had a fiery nature to match her tresses, and fear filled him when he thought about all the ways one could torture another. Edmund was more terrified by the knowledge her character wouldn't take to being forced into anything; no, she wouldn't be meek and mild, and that might lead her to death's doorway.

Edmund was at the door in an instant. His fingers curled around the cool metal of the knob, gently twisting and pulling the door open. He left his chamber and found his way to a grand room where he was surrounded by fantastical creatures that even his wildest imagination had never fathomed. Horns, tails, hooves, and all matter of animal features were on display for his widened eyes. There were beings that nearly stole the breath from his body as their twisted features caught his notice. And, of course, there were faeries that delighted his senses with how very beautiful they were. He was an artist with a whimsical soul and felt drawn to create their likeness in wood. Too bad he lacked wood to whittle; the activity would settle his fraying nerves. Though for him, none could quite touch the beauty his Faetilda possessed. His fingers twitched at his sides to sculpt her image from the ebony wood. Edmund felt the eyes of many taking him in as he shyly crept into the room. Finding a chair, he made himself comfortable; there was nothing he could do to sway the decision being made. He was just an interloper in their midst. *Human* and *mortal* were among the most filthy words they knew.

Quietly, Edmund listened to Finnius and his comrades as they formed a plan to raid the entire castle and raze it to the ground in a brilliant show of defiance. He wasn't abhorrent to the idea, although to go through the entire palace successfully, would be rather difficult. Edmund's heart was adamant in the desire to comb room by room, together and undivided, until they found Faetilda and the other poor souls. Though he suspected it wouldn't be that simple, not with the army, the queen commanded.

The palace was rumored to house hidden passages and chambers. How were they to successfully search them all? The best way forward was to allow Finnius and his elite tracking skills to lead them, find where Faetilda was, rescue the others, and then abscond back to Faerie. Shouts and jeers filled the air as each powerful faerie made their own wishes known.

When he could stay mute no longer, Edmond tentatively raised his hand into the air and cleared his throat. Heads snapped in his direction. When the gaze of a fae whose silver eyes narrowed at him with hate marked on his curled lips, Edmund felt as if a pound of sand had been deposited in his mouth. Clearing his throat, he made his suggestion. "We are wasting time and need to settle on a permanent decision, as I could not endure another night without knowing Faetilda's fate."

"We must do as Edmund suggests," Finnius declared, rising from his seat. "I shall track her scent since she was the last to be taken, and her scent will still be the strongest. But to attack headlong is pure folly."

"Our kin have been estranged from us long enough!" barked a snarling wolf. "Blood for blood is the only way."

"There are other ways," Flora admonished. "I agree with dear Edmund and Finnius. We must be tactical."

Edmund nodded, feeling emboldened by his new friend's support of him. "First, we need to discover Faetilda's scent. It's imperative to locate where she is within Buckingham House. I have an idea, but I'm altogether not entirely certain. Once we know where she is, we raid the palace, unbinding and saving everyone. We do not stray from this. We must all make it out and back over the wall before dawn."

Finnius nodded at him, respect shining from his eyes. Flora gave Edmund a brittle smile. The tense faces of those surrounding him spoke of their trepidation. Not that he blamed his companions. He, too, was resolute in saving Faetilda and was scared of failing all the same. It was a monumental endeavor and the chances of succeeding were not great. They had brawn, and he hoped a good deal of intellect to ascertain what needed to be accomplished moment by moment.

Edmund glanced outside, noting the setting rose-gold sun splashing the teal skies in a radiance of color. He'd never before seen a sunset more magnificent, and the pain of longing seared his heart; Faetilda should be sharing the view with him. It was time to act, even if he was the only one to climb over the wall. Let the others continue to squabble if they must, but he was on the path that destiny had set before him. Striding to the cloak hanger by the door, Edmund grabbed a gray cape, shrugging it over his shoulders. He buttoned the wool garment up near his chin. Behind him, chairs screeched back on the hardwood floors. Grunts and grumbles of agreement to get going this very instant permeated the thick air.

Peeking up, Maggery stood before him, draping a navy scarf around his neck. "'Tis mighty cold over The Wall," she stated, locking her gaze with his. "Bring her back."

With a resolute nod, Edmund strode out the door with Finnius hot on his heels. The shifter strode in front of him, his every inch commanding veneration, leading the way to The Wall. Numerous shifters, faerie beings, ogres, trolls, and a host of others came treading out of the meeting. Edmund peered around, noting they all carried a varying degree of weapons, but all wore faces of angered determination. The sight set his pulse to racing. These were kindred friends.

This trip through the woods was speedily accomplished. His ears perked up with the caroling of the bells, ringing a victorious melody as they marched on, united in their resolution to reign terror on their oppressors and to gain their loved ones back. Edmund harbored no doubt this mission would be anything short of dangerous.

Chapter Twelve

Do You Hear What I Hear?

The bone-chilling cold from the tiny barred window above Faetilda's head made her body shiver and sent icy tendrils up and down her spine. The tiny cell, not even six paces wide, was entirely dank and bitterly cold. There was no possible way to hide from the dampness leaching through her clothing and encasing her heart in frost. Every burst of the biting wind shot daggers along her skin and stole her breath. Faetilda curled her body atop the stone floor and tried to rub warmth into her bound limbs. It was a fruitless activity, and she couldn't keep the trembling away. Her thoughts circled back to Edmund, her friends, and Faerie. Anything to take her mind from the reality that was slowly driving her mad.

From outside her prison, the wails of those in torment and the harsh words of their captors plagued her splintered nerves. She wanted to cover her ears and hum all the discording notes away, to lose herself in the autonomy of her future that wasn't bleak and frightening.

Her tired mind must have sought slumber because when cruel hands began to wrest her to wakefulness, she thought she was back in Faerie with the trolls for a moment. The punishing kick to her ribs was an unmistakable reminder of where she was. Lights exploded behind her eyes as her breath came out in an anguished cry.

"Get up, you rotten cabbage! The queen awaits your inspection," jeered a man whose black and decaying teeth set in a bloodthirsty sneer hovered above her.

She used her hands to push herself to her feet, and the pain in her side nearly had her sprawled before his feet again. Only sheer willpower kept her upright as she let the guard grab hold of the rope, and pulled her from the cell. The light from the wall torches was too much for her delicate eyes, and she had to blink as she stumbled along on her injured ankle after the vile human. Tears made her vision hazy, and she didn't care that she fluttered them from her eyes. What were her tears to such barbarians as these?

Exiting the double doors to the hidden penitentiary, they left the grunts and weeping behind. Though she knew other guards were staring at her, they left her alone, and she was content to watch the floor they walked upon. Faetilda was escorted between the walls and through the corridors, then through more hidden recesses until they came to an ornate set of double doors. The lush throne room was decorated in rich scarlet and golden furnishings and accent pieces. Only a few armchairs were placed by the sides of the royal seats and on those resided ladies clad in muslin and satin. A grand chandelier aflame with glittering ivory candles was suspended above, while the moldings and plasters along the room's ceiling and edges vied for attention. But the focal point of the throne room was the queen. Perched atop one of the thrones was a slight woman drenched in ivory and with ostrich feathers that bobbed and weaved with every motion she made. Her dark eyes latched onto Faetilda, her intrusive gaze sweeping from the faerie's head to the boots on her feet. Once they reached the sovereign, the officer shoved Faetilda in the middle of her back, sending her crashing to her knees. Faetilda didn't feel the pain; her legs had gone too numb in the cold cell. Dropping her gaze to the floor before her, Faetilda remained still and silent.

"My, what a pretty thing you are," Queen Charlotte said.

Thing, not a faerie, not even a person. As if her value was nothing more than a button on a glove. Anger, hot and fierce, lit her core with the desire to lash out, but Faetilda drew her emotions in, locking them away in her heart.

"You have nothing to say, *faerie*?" the queen prompted.

Faetilda's head was wrenched upward by the traumatizing force of the queen's defender. His fingers dug half-moon indentations along the supple skin of her jaw.

"That's better, wretch. Don't you know respect is due to me? That's the real issue with you *creatures*: you have no appreciation for your betters. Still," she paused to observe the faerie before her again, peering intently at her crushed wings. "You do possess great beauty; what a boon to my collection you shall be!"

The ladies in waiting softly applauded Queen Charlotte's declaration.

"Rupert, have her cleaned and handed over to the director of my menagerie. She'll be thrilling to behold next to my lions and peacocks.

Remove the fae that dwells there now, exterminate him if you must but," she lifted a hand with her palm outspread and continued, "be merciful and make it a dignified ending. After all, the creature was quite adept at illusions and entertaining my court."

Revulsion and horror made Faetilda's heart race and a cold sweat dampened the hairs at the back of her neck. She knew these savages cared little for her kind, but hearing the very casual conversation about killing one of her kin threatened all of her carefully controlled feelings. If she cried now, the tears wouldn't be hopeless; they'd be murderous. Every horrible tale she'd ever heard about this realm held more merit and weight in her mind.

"As you wish, Your Majesty," Rupert's simpering voice annoyed all the nerve endings in Faetilda's body, what she wouldn't give to rear up and elbow him in his naughty bits. But she had to use her wits and attempt to gain her freedom from the iron bars of her prison. She began to feel some semblance of strength returning to her.

Rupert let her chin go, and she moved it back and forth to restore the feeling. Rupert reached down and, with a pain-filled tug of her tresses, restored Faetilda to her tottering feet.

"Gently, Ruppert, gently," scolded Queen Charlotte. "We aren't monsters, are we?"

"No, my queen," he said, then bowed before he backed away, drawing Faetilda along with him.

Her boot heels dragged across the carpeted floor. She allowed her weakened limbs to hang as she gathered the strength for what would come next. Faetilda's heart held no qualms about leveling this palace to the ground, and she would do so when the chance presented itself. She would make these mortals suffer and endure the fates that had been so easily handed to her kind. There wouldn't be another wintertide where the fae dwelled beneath the boots of these humans to nonchalantly squash at will.

Exiting the throne room, Rupert held her firmly by her forearm as he, once again, led Faetilda through a secret passage. On the other side were a series of doors, and he took her through the second one to the right.

The dimly lit chamber was washed in brilliant jade hues with an ivory dressing table, a matching satin-padded bench, and a rose-adorned looking glass carved with exquisite petals. The very middle of the room contained a copper tub with wisps of curling steam rising from its surface. Faetilda cringed at the water. She hated getting her wings wet. They were already so damaged from her mistreatment, and she hoped the hot liquid wouldn't further injure them. Giving her translucent wings a delicate pump, Faetilda's back spasmed, and she flinched as a million tiny knives stabbed her with vicious brutality.

A petite golden-haired maid garbed in black came bustling through a doorway Faetilda hadn't yet noticed. Her curious blue eyes landed on the faerie, and she tilted her head. "My, you are a wreck; what have these brutes done to you?" The compassion in the maid's tone and the furrowing of her brow threatened to cause all of Faetilda's vaulted feelings to flee from her.

"Her Majesty wants this faerie looking her best and placed into the menagerie post haste." Rupert glared at the maid and, giving Faetilda one last cruel squeeze along her arm, relinquished his hold.

Hearing the door shut behind her was one of the most relieving sounds Faetilda's ears had ever heard. Thick knots of tension unwound, leaving her feeling drained and weary.

"Here now, dearie, I won't harm you," the maid said as she came forward, encircling Faetilda's waist.

Faetilda wasn't certain if it was hearing the endearment that Flora often addressed her by or the tender actions of the human, but something in her heart warmed, and she immediately felt a well of kindness filling up in her being. This was a mortal who possessed a soul just as bright and lovely as her Edmund's. Whatever happened, she'd take care to ensure this maid wasn't caught in the crossfire, for Faetilda meant to enact her rage on those who deserved it.

Once she was scrubbed clean and soaking in the tub, Faetilda reached for her magic. It was still there, but only a minuscule flicker remained. She had burnt the majority of it earlier on her failed escape attempt. She wouldn't be so careless again.

"Let's get you dry and settled before the fire," the servant said, holding a towel before Faetilda.

After rising and being dried off, she was seated before the undulating orange flames. Her fiery hair was hanging loosely down her back, drying at a snail's pace. From behind her, the sounds of the woman readying things for her drew her attention.

"What's your name?" Faetilda asked timidly.

"Beverly, and yours?"

"You've got a lovely name. Mine is Faetilda." Canting her head, she took in the mossy green ball gown Beverly was arranging atop an armchair. Was she to wear that? It looked as if it had cost a small fortune.

"You have a most unusual name. Is it uncommon to have 'fae' in your name?"

"It's not uncommon at all," Faetilda replied as she rose to her bare feet and padded over to the gown, which boasted tiny bows along the hemline and lace at the bodice. This realm did have a fabulous sense of fashion, and though the dress wasn't life or death, a small part of her thrilled at the fact she would soon don it.

Beverly directed Faetilda over to the dressing table and began to brush her hair, then twisted it into a knot with flowing curls that dangled along the nape of her neck and framed her face. Pearl-tipped pins were used to secure the fiery tresses in place. Next, the towel was discarded, and she was dressed in underthings, silk slippers, and the gorgeous ball gown, which glided over her shoulders and down her body. The faerie's damaged wings peeked from hidden slits in the folds of the material. The fabric shimmered like diamonds in the sun with every shift Faetilda made. The tiny buttons along her back took an age to fasten, but when the task was done, Beverly paraded her in front of the long rosewood-looking glass. A gasp left Faetilda's mouth as she twirled in place, her eyes never leaving the mossy material.

"You look divine!" Beverly smiled at her, her blue eyes soft and kind.

A smile played about Faetilda's lips, but it was marred by the broken shards of her heart as she tried to fortify herself for her induction behind glass walls. She was lovely, but the joy at her appearance faded as she felt more and more insignificant. What did it matter what she wore, how lovely her hair or clothing was, if she existed solely to delight the eye? Her wings were still hanging limply behind her, and she worried they would never be the same again.

Beverly guided her to the door, allowing her to pass through the doorway first. Rupert scowled at her, took her by the arm, and led her down the hallway; their footsteps reverberated off the walls, sounding in her heart like a death march.

Beverly halted them with widened eyes as she turned to meet Rupert's stare. "Do you hear what I hear?"

Perking her ears, Faetilda caught the clash of struggle and the dissonance of a battle. Hope soared on battered wings as euphoria rushed through her veins, making her determined to join in the fray. Faetilda wrenched her arm free of Rupert's hold. Lifting her slippered foot, she landed a blow against Rupert's stomach, sending him careening to the floor. Not wasting a moment, she gathered the volume of her hemline and then dashed down the corridor with Beverly close on her heels and shouting.

Chapter Thirteen

Here We Come A-wassailing

"Faetilda!" Edmund hollered as his eyes took in every movement in the dimly lit corridor.

Edmund's sword collided with the enemy directly in his path, slicing clean through the man's shoulder. The queen's guard screamed, collapsing to the ground. Faetilda was near; Edmund felt her in his heart; some invisible tether was joining his soul to hers.

Their forces continued marching deeper inside the Queen's House. Finding the others in the dungeon was an easy enough rescue. Finding Faetilda had become a more troublesome task, and each step was a struggle to keep his panic in check.

Finnius rushed down another long hallway. Members of their squad matched his frantic pace. Edmund shot after him, unwilling to lose the shifter, and his best lead to locating Faetilda. Together, their group paused on the threshold of a double-wide gilded oak door. Finnius sniffed the wood and lowered his nose to the floor.

"She's been here recently," he said, charging through the doors.

The queen's guards poured out of the room like a torrent of rain from the sky during a summer storm. Edmund's sword collided with the body of an officer, impaling the man through his middle. He shoved the dying guard aside, taking on another foe. His eyes crossed to his tin soldiers, who were following his order and cutting their enemy down in neat strikes. Edmund had never before felt so proud of the usefulness of his creations. In between the clanging of metal, he called Faetilda's name. Could she even hear him above the clamor of weapon upon weapon and moans of the wounded?

His sword sliced through the chest of another as if the blade was enchanted. Edmund whirled around; his eyes narrowed to slits as he ended a guard who had Finnius pinned to the ground. A bright zap of magic flew past him, narrowly missing his ear. Pivoting on his heels, Edmund spied Flora. At the very back of their ranks, she was aiding those she could with her golden magic and defending those too weak from imprisonment to fight back.

Those they rescued, who were able, picked up weapons from the fallen as they charged forward to enact their revenge. Agonized cries permeated the chaotic air. The din of weapons clashing and sparks flying was enough to give Edmund a slight pause. *So much death.* This was never what he wanted, but it was clear it was an unavoidable part of the pathway to freedom. For who would ever seek to capture the fae again after this massacre?

A Queen's Man advanced from his right, commanding his focus. Edmund spun on his heel, whipping the blade around to counter the impending blow. His arm throbbed from the contact of their colliding weapons. Edmund wheeled about, kicking the man in the back and sending him careening to the floor. A fae stepped in, finishing the man off.

Glancing up, Edmund saw an antlered fae with glimmering, green, gossamer wings charge past him. Edmund felt for the being, having literally just saved him from a guillotine and an atrocious beheading. Edmund charged behind him toward their intended target. The Queen's Man raised his sword, the weapon trembling in his hands as sputtered words fell from his lips. Like a crashing of a wave, they took out the entire throne room of officers, unstoppable in their justice.

Edmund dashed through the slain bodies and puddles of blood toward the first door he saw. Ripping it open, his eyes scanned the contents of the dark passageway for her.

"Faetilda!" he yelled, pausing long enough to hear nothing in return.

Finnius came up beside him, sniffing the air. "She was in here not a moment ago."

The statement gave Emdund's heart a lurch as he swallowed. She must be safe and well!

His friend rushed past him with sword drawn and a menacing scowl across his features, ferreting out which direction Faetilda was taken.

"Hurry, Beloved," Flora urged with barely restrained panic in her tone.

"This way!" Finnius bellowed, opening a door and bursting through.

Edmund rushed after the man. Passing through just a second behind him, Edmund nearly collided with a halted Finnius. Edmund's eyes scanned the chamber. Faetilda was kneeling in the middle of a group of queen's guards. Eight sharp-tipped swords were pointed at her throat, and a rivulet of crimson trailed down her creamy skin. Tears seeped down from her amethyst eyes, staining her cheeks.

Edmund rushed forward but was stopped by Finnius's heavy hand. Edmund's blood roiled in his veins as his face mottled in fury.

"Drop your weapons!" a dark-haired Queen's Man demanded.

"Not likely," Edmund snarled.

"Very well," he sneered. "If you do not drop your weapons, her pretty throat will have a sword cleaving it from shoulder to shoulder."

The clatter of the tin soldier's boots stopped, and Edmund turned his head to observe them.

"What in all the realm's sake are these monstrosities?" the leader of the human officers asked as his eyes widened with fright.

"They are *my men*," Edmund answered as his chest puffed out with pride.

Flora struggled her way past the fingertips of her friends, eyes narrowed on the human leader who spoke. She wriggled in her dress, pushing the sleeves up as her glare intensified. Finnius held out his arm, prohibiting her from striding forward.

A butterfly fae with shimmering purple wings came to stand beside Flora. The dark-skinned fae whirled one hand over the other, creating a purple orb. Flora did the same with her hands, creating her own golden orb. Together, the two orbs merged. One by one, the fae came up to Flora, creating another orb, depositing each one atop the others and backing away.

The queen's guards stared wide-eyed and slack-jawed at the unbelievable display of magic that was waiting to be unleashed on them.

Another faerie moved to Flora's side and began to hum in an eerily haunting tone, making the tiny hairs along Edmund's arm rise. Tingles from the magic humming inside the orb made him shudder in anticipation.

Each one of the gapping officers' arms fell to their sides. Their swords clattered carelessly to the ground. The singing fae's melody rose to a faster tempo. The bird-like fae smiled venomously, her voice lilting and dropping.

Edmund inched his way closer to Faetilda. She slowly gained her feet, slipping away from the distracted men whose eyes were glazed over. Edmund's heart thundered in his chest. Her amethyst eyes stared into his, searching, though Edmund could not meet her gaze. He was too unsettled to offer her reassurance and security until she was fully enfolded in his arms. His hands took hold of her bound ones, gently pulling her toward him.

The fae continued singing, continuing the same unearthly enchanting song. Edmund tugged Faetilda forward into the folds of her kin, setting his back precariously to the officers. Whipping the sheathed knife from his side, he cut her horrid bonds away.

Faetilda smiled, teardrops slipping unburdened from her eyes. Edmund took her in his arms, holding her tightly against him. His fingers wove into her soft tresses. He breathed out, thankful to have finally found her.

"We must hurry now, friends," cautioned Flora and happy tears swam in her vision as she looked at Faetilda. "We can't contain the orbs forever."

Edmund sheathed his knife. Adjusting the sword in his right hand, he took Faetilda's hand in his left, lacing her fingers with his. A warm smile split his face. The melding of their hands felt like the mending of his heart. Was there anything more pure than the bond of a new love forming?

The bird-like fae snapped her beak shut, ending the beautiful song. The dull-witted officers were released from their trance. The men scrambled for their weapons. Edmund's eyes widened. While he was focused on sneaking Faetilda out of their hold, a dozen more had taken up arms behind the initial circle of eight.

"Go!" Flora urged, struggling to contain the ball of magic that was pulsating at an alarming rate.

The others dashed back out the door. Edmund, with Faetilda in tow, brought up the rear. Finnius grabbed Flora's arm just as she shot the giant ball of magic at the men. Edmund pushed Faetilda forward, taking a step back to push Flora through the door. Once the ladies were through, Edmund and Finnius grabbed for the door, trying to force it closed in time. Edmund's eyes widened as he watched through the slit in the doorway; the magic exploded upon contact, and the force sent the men careening backward, engulfed in metallic flames.

"We can't go back the way we came. It will be crawling with guards," Edmund stated, retaking Faetilda's hand. She was now his lifeline.

"I don't know this castle. You don't either, so what do you suggest?" Finnius retorted, his bushy brows furrowed.

Edmund shrugged. "Shall we jump out a window?"

Finnius smirked. "I'm beginning to like you."

Faetilda tested her wings and announced, "I believe that I have just enough left in me to soften the landing."

"Perfect. And I shall aid in *softening the landing* just in case, my dear," Flora beamed, laying a gentle hand atop her friend's forearm to soothe her.

"Let's fly." The singing fae smiled, creating another magical orb and hurling it forward to break the throne room's stained glass window.

"By the Creator, we're really doing this," Edmund stammered as his heart palpitated.

"It's not terrible," Finnius smirked.

"Oh yes, nothing terrible about leaping to one's death!"

Finnius's booming laughter filled the room. "You suggested it."

"I'll never suggest a thing again." Edmund sighed and shook his head.

Faetilda tittered, shrugging her shoulders. "Faith, trust, and faerie dust," she yelled, yanking Edmund by his cravat and leaping out the window.

Edmund couldn't make his eyes close. In horror, he stared down at the ground, holding the last biting breath of fresh air in his lungs. Faetilda's rose-gold gossamer wings fluttered valiantly, trying to slow their fall. Somehow, she was able to manage the task of decelerating their momentum with a few well-timed pumps of her battered wings, averting their impending deaths.

"I have you," Flora said, using her magic to blow a pile of snow under them.

With an *oomph*, they landed in the magicked mound of snow. The sudden sensation of dampness crept into his clothing and made him shudder violently.

Edmund peeled one eye open, scanning the ground around them. Everyone had made it out safely, which had seemed an impossible feat at the beginning of the evening. Slowly and still under the cover of darkness, the others were swiping the snow from their heads and faces, making their way out of the palace grounds. Edmund scrambled to his feet, dusting the snow off of himself. He found his sword, which was sticking straight up from the snow pile. His brows puckered as he considered it and wondered if he'd ever have a cause to use it again. Gingerly, he plucked it from its resting place.

"When we get back to Faerie, I'm not going outdoors for a week," Faetilda said, struggling to pull herself from the deep snow mound.

"I wouldn't mind that at all either," Edmund replied, reaching down and helping Faetilda to her feet.

Taking her hand, they ran together toward The Wall, never looking back. They didn't see the glowering eyes of the Lord Darlington, who stood amidst the shadows, a silent witness to what had transpired.

Chapter Fourteen

I Saw Faerie Kissing a Human

The light of the new day stained the human world in brilliant orange light as the faeries, trolls, ogres, tin soldiers, and Edmund stood before the wall. Looking over his shoulder, Edmund's eyes seemed to drink their fill of his world one last time. It wasn't a question of remaining here; he couldn't. He would never be safe, and now that Faetilda had had a taste of their hands woven together, she couldn't ever let him go. In fact, she turned to Flora at her side and whispered into her ear. A delighted smile broke out across her friend's face, and she happily handed over her golden wand.

Meeting Edmund's eyes, Faetilda gave him a demure smile and said, "We can't leave your toy shoppe to some other. It simply must come with us!" With a wave of her borrowed wand, she cast golden stars that leaped into the air and shimmered their way over the horizon.

"What do you mean to do?" The perplexed look on Edmund's features made a giggle soar through her.

"At first, I had thought what merry fun it would be to have your stuffed animals and dolls come parading down the streets with all your other marvelous inventions closely behind. But then, the thought of how terrifying that might be to the pesky mortals who can't stomach magic made me rethink just a bit. If your beautiful creations came to ruin again because of me, I don't think my heart could bear it. So this will be much better!" Faetilda switched her attention to the residents of Faerie, who were busily climbing over The Wall. When it was just her and Edmund who remained, she felt a sudden attack of shyness settle into the pit of her stomach as if bumble bees zipped along inside.

Edmund reached a hand toward a wayward lock of her hair, carefully tucking it back behind her ear; his rough fingertips against the sensitive flesh behind her ear caused the breath in her lungs to hitch.

A low chuckle escaped from between Edmund's lips, and her heart skipped a beat. "I do believe we've scandalized London enough for one evening," he said.

"Do you not agree with the actions taken tonight?" The thought he regretted any part in securing her freedom was like a dagger twisting in her heart.

"Not when it comes to your well-being. Let me make that perfectly clear. I...wasn't myself when I learned you had been taken and couldn't concentrate on anything that didn't lead to bringing you back to Faerie. I only hope you won't grow tired of this old man," he said as he looked down at his slush-covered boots.

At that, she reached for his face. Delicately, she placed her palm against his stubbled cheek, which was bitterly chilled. Staring into his gray eyes, she almost forgot what it was she wanted to say. "Edmund, you silly human. It would be impossible for me to ever become weary of your presence in my life. You probably don't understand the ways of Faerie and how—"

"You mean the part about us being Fated Mates?" he interrupted as her hand dropped from his face.

A gasp flew from her parted lips. "How did you learn about that?"

"Flora and Finnius."

"Oh. Of course, they would step in and reveal that." Her stomach sank as disappointment mounted, almost crushing her under a crashing wave of uncertainty.

"That upsets you?" His voice sounded confused.

"Yes and no. I had hoped to discover whether you held any tender feeling for me before we got into the whole Mate complication." She wrung her hands together.

"Is it complicated?" His brows arched.

"Isn't it? I mean, you're mortal. I'm not. It seems as if we're natural enemies."

Edmund captured her free hand, turning her palm upward. His warm lips descended to her skin in a feather-light kiss that made her insides dance with glee and warmth rush from her head to her limbs in delicious waves.

"Does it feel like we're enemies? I mean, I don't have any pointy teeth," he asked with a roguish smirk.

"That you do not," she replied, grinning.

Edmund held her close, kissing the top of her head. "Any mortal time I have left with you is time well spent."

Faetilda beamed at him. "You'll age more slowly in Faerie. So we shall have many years together."

"Wonderful years with *you* by my side."

Words had completely flown from Faetilda's mind, and she had lost the ability to even think. Shaking her head, she allowed the storm of her feelings to coalesce in her chest. She had been through so much; the fact he wanted her, too, was everything she had never allowed herself to dream or dare hope for. A torrent of tears coursed down her cheeks as she bowed her head against his solid chest. He held her, making soothing noises, placing gentle kisses atop her upswept coiffure. Faetilda had never felt so treasured, so cared for in her entire—

The rumble of a laugh obliterated her heart. Was she ridiculous to him after all? Tearing her head away from him, she looked up to see where his stare was affixed. A dark object became clearly visible in a sky that was now quickly filling with snow-laden clouds. Faerie Wishes was making its way home.

"I know I heard you correctly before, but what a sight it is indeed to see my shoppe hovering over our heads." His joyful laugh restored her heart and good humor.

"What amusement we will have fashioning toys for all of Faerie! Just think of all the troll boys, girls, and ogres that your creations will bring joy to. We can hire some of your toy soldiers to help you fulfill all the varied requests, and, of course, I will be right by your side, helping where I may."

"I'm a man and must make my own way."

"And so you shall."

Faetilda rose to her tiptoes and placed her lips against Edmund's. It took a moment for his enthusiastic response to take hold. Between their two bodies, a tiny golden light flickered into being and ribboned itself from her heart to his, linking their souls together forever more.

Epilogue

Very Merry Faerie Wishes

Several weeks later or perhaps mere days…? The passage of time was so difficult to pin down in Faerie. Edmund wouldn't trade a day away for anything. He was living amongst the fae creatures, evermore tied to the love of his life and building toys every hour of the day. Well, except for today, which was Christmastide for a long time. Whether human or something more, the joy in a young one's eyes would never stop delighting him.

He was standing in the cottage, which he and Faetilda were turning into a little bit more of a home each day. Before the fireplace was a pine tree with dozens of flickering candles, their blue flames wavering but never catching the branches on fire. Gold and silver bells nested in the greenery, and presents sat under the lowest limbs. His heart had never been so full before; he hadn't shared a holiday's warmth with any since he was a lad. Later this afternoon, he'd host a cottageful as Flora and Finnius, along with their troll charges, came to dine. He couldn't wait to see how the trolls liked the toys he had made with them in mind.

"Come look out the window, my love!" Faetilda waved her hand to beckon him over to her side.

Crossing to her, he threaded their fingers together and pressed a kiss to her temple. It was astounding that he, a mere mortal, could bring the prettiest fae to a blush. He reveled in the small amount of power he possessed.

Forcing his eyes to leave her lovely face, he leaned forward to peer out the window. Down the lane, his soldiers were pulling sleighs overbrimming with faerielings, who shouted their jubilation amidst the swirling snowflakes. His gentle giants never displayed an ounce of malice and were very good with the little ones, who seemed to adore them. Edmund had no doubt if trouble ever crossed into Faerie, his tin men would be the first wave of defense. And he would certainly take up arms again to defend the happy home he cherished.

"Do you suppose you'd like to be a father one day?"

The question almost knocked Edmund to the floor. He stared at his Fated Mate as he tried to figure out what exactly she meant. *He, a father?* That was preposterous. Wasn't it? The little seed was swallowed up by his heart and began to flourish. A father, indeed. Well, why not?

"I think it's a lovely idea! When shall we begin the process?" he teased, as he drew her away from the window and over to the cream settee to settle down in his lap.

With the glow of the fireplace, the glass trinkets atop the mantle cast rainbowed light along the wooden floorboards. With the distant sound of carolers and his one true love in his arms, Edmund had never felt so enchanted before. Well, except for the night a certain faerie visited his toy shoppe, Faerie Wishes.

About: Michelle Helen Fritz

Michelle Helen Fritz was born in Maryland and raised in Arizona with lots of traveling throughout the States. She began her literary career as a personal assistant to Indie authors and loves to see the process of an idea turn into a finished book. Michelle loves to write about dashing heroes and the compelling women that tempt them with a dash of intrigue, an abundant amount of romance, and scenes that hopefully make her readers swoon. She is the mother of four children whom she homeschools and currently resides in Maryland with her own jaunty hero who makes all of her dreams come true.

You can follow Michelle on:

Amazon Author Page: Michelle Helen Fritz

Facebook: Author Michelle Helen Fritz

Instagram: Author Michelle Helen Fritz

Acknowledgements

Michelle Helen Fritz

First of all, thank you to YOU! You took a chance on this book, and I am forever grateful for that.

Thank you to my Handsome Hubby as well as to my littles. You make every day an adventure.

Thank you so very much to Wanderlust Ink & Tomb L.L.C. for creating such a fabulous cover!

Brittany, the bestest PA ever: You rock. Thank you for all the things!

Thank you so very much to Cathey for all the polish you gave to this short story. It wouldn't be the same without your diligence and dedication.

A huge thank you to J.J. Marshall for just being so amazing and supportive. You are such a treasure!

And thank you to my Creator. Every imagination needs some inspiration. Thank you for bestowing me with the gifts I have.

Also by: Michelle Helen Fritz

A Bramley Hall Regency Romance

Love At Last

Love That Lasts

Love Ever Lasting

Shades of Bramley Hall Regency Romance

Love Holds True

Courts & Curses

A Court Of Broken Dreams and Curse

A Court of Broken Promises and Nightmares

A Court of Broken Hopes and Wishes

Paullett Golden Anthology

Hourglass Romance: *Love At Rescue*

Romantic Choices: *Love Flames Anew*

Romantic Realms Anthology

Hearts At War: *Faerie Boots*

Shifting Hearts: *Faeriely Tart*

Beyond The Depths Anthology

A Bite of Winter & A Sip of Trouble: *Faerie Wishes*

About: E.A. Shanniak

E.A. (Ericka Ashlee) Shanniak is the author of several successful series – A Castre World Novel – Whitman Western Romances – Dangerous Ties. She's hobbit-sized, barely reaching over 5ft tall on a good day. When she wears her Ariat boots, not only does she gain an inch, she's then able to reach the kitchen cabinets to get all the snacks. When not in her fox den (writing cave), Ericka loves to spend time with her family – outside having firepits with wine, camping, fishing, or zooming in her jeep on another Midwest adventure. Ericka loves all the animals her kids bring home including numerous barn cats and their newfound duck named Delilah.

Ericka works in the Register of Deeds office residing in a small town in Comanche County with her supportive, wonderful husband, two amazingly compassionate kids, and all the animals (including those her husband knows nothing about yet). Follow her on her Kansas adventures with these social media platforms listed below.

- Facebook

- Facebook group: Shanniak Shenanigans
- Instagram

website: http://www.eashanniak.com/
email: erickashanniak@gmail.com

If have a moment, I would really appreciate a review. A review, whether you liked it or not, helps me know what aspects of the story you liked. Even a rating is helpful. Thank you so much for reading my work. I hope you have a fabulous day.

Also by: E.A. Shanniak

Alien Prince Reverse Harem – Ubsolvyn District:

Stalking Death - *prequel*

Securing Freedom

Saving Home

Bayonet Books Anthology:

Storming Area 51: *Stalking Death*

Slay Bells Ring: *Stocking Gryla*

Beyond The Depths Anthology

A Bite of Winter & A Sip of Trouble: *Faerie Wishes*

Clean Fantasy Romance – Zerelon World Novella:

Aiding Azlyn

Killing Karlyn

Reviving Roslyn

Clean & Sweet Regency Romance – Bramley Hall:

Love At Last
Love That Lasts
Love Ever Lasting

Clean & Sweet Western Romance – Whitman Western Series:

To Find A Whitman
To Love A Thief
To Save A Life
To Lift A Darkness
To Veil A Fondness
To Bind A Heart
To Hide A Treasure
To Want A Change
To Form A Romance

Harlequin Fantasy Romance – Castre World Novel:

Piercing Jordie
Mitering Avalee
Forging Calida
Uplifting Irie
Braving Evan
Warring Devan
Hunting Megan
Shifting Aramoren – *short story*
Anchoring Nola – *short story*

Paullett Golden Anthology:

Hourglass Romance: *Love At Rescue*
Romantic Choices: *Love Flames Anew*

Romantic Realms Anthology
Shifting Hearts: *Faeriely Tart*

Slow Burn Enemies to Lovers Paranormal Romance – Dangerous Ties:
Opening Danger
Hunting Danger
Burning Danger

Slow Burn Enemies to Lovers Paranormal Romance – Wicked Ties:
Wicked Witch
Wicked Bonds
Wicked Ruin

Standalone Stories:
Winter Luna

www.ingramcontent.com/pod-product-compliance
Lightning Source LLC
Chambersburg PA
CBHW070550310726
48982CB00011B/1526/J

* 9 7 9 8 9 9 0 3 8 1 1 6 2 *